M000034650

SNOW AND OTHER FOUR-LETTER WORDS

KIT EARNSHAW

Copyright © 2022 by Kit Earnshaw

All rights reserved.

No part of this book may be reproduced in any form or by any electronic or mechanical means, including information storage and retrieval systems, without written permission from the author, except for the use of brief quotations in a book review.

This is a work of fiction. Any resemblance to actual events or persons, living or dead, is entirely coincidental.

ISBN: 978-1-7369771-4-9

First Edition

Chapter 1

I KNEW IT WAS ALL GOING DOWNHILL WHEN I FLEW across country to help my best friend Kelsey move post-divorce. Little did I realize, though, that there would be very real downhill slopes in my near future. I thought I would just be helping a friend through a tough time, but, *of course*, the universe had bigger plans for me. I had no idea just how much my life was about to change when I left my busy, bustling New York City for the pristine snow-banks and cozy charm of Moose Creek, Colorado.

"I can't *believe* you convinced me to help you move," I said with a grunt. My arms strained against a bulging cardboard box as I walked care-fully towards to the moving truck. Kelsey had a habit of talking me into things I didn't want to do.

"*I* can't believe you let me marry that asshole,"

Kelsey said, her arms wrapped around a loaded cardboard box. She swayed, struggling from its weight as she lugged it out to the U-Haul.

I let out a playful laugh. "I mean, we tried to warn you, Kels," I repeated for the millionth time, following her with my own overstuffed box. This one was labeled MISC. BABY in bold sharpie. It was a conversation we'd been having on a loop for the past five years.

Kelsey sighed as she dropped the box, perching on the edge of the truck. "God, I was pretty stubborn, wasn't I?"

"Stubborn's a nice way to put it." Kelsey knew I was teasing. She had screamed at me and the rest of our friends at her Bachelorette weekend in Miami when we tried to talk to her about our concerns. Rick, the man she married and now just divorced, was a condescending prick. Rich and accomplished, maybe, but a condescending prick, nonetheless.

"Thanks for helping me, Annie."

I sat down next to her, slinging my arm around her shoulders. Kelsey leaned into me and rested her chin on my shoulder.

"I'll always be here for you, Kels. You know that." Kelsey and I had been friends since third grade. I'd say best friends, but that sounded so juvenile and reductive for what we meant to each other.

Kelsey was my sister; she was family. I'd grown up with an older brother, Will, but Kelsey was an only child. We'd become chosen family.

"And everything's gonna be okay," I added. She nodded but didn't look convinced. "*I mean it*—it's gonna be okay. You're better off without him."

She sighed. "I know, I know. It's just a big . . . change."

"Change can be good." I said it, but I didn't know if I believed it. Who was I to say *change* was good? Kelsey and I could both be stubborn in our own ways. I knew what I liked and what I didn't like. I knew what my limits were, and I didn't like them to be challenged.

"I'm gonna miss this house." We sat in silence, admiring the large house facing us. Nicer than anything I'd ever lived in. Palatial compared to my tiny studio apartment in the city, with the bathroom door you could only close if you lifted the toilet lid because it was such a tight space. I couldn't imagine living in a house as grand as the one Kelsey was now leaving. Five bedrooms, a master bathroom with a steam shower, a heated pool in the backyard, a private tennis court—it was luxe. And Kelsey was definitely downsizing. She was moving into a quaint (for her, at least) two-bedroom townhouse near Moose Creek, where she'd miraculously procured her old job on the ski resort's events team.

I DROVE THE U-HAUL DOWN THE WINDING mountain roads towards Kelsey's new house. She sat beside me in the passenger's seat, humming along to the radio as we watched the mountains grow taller. The midday sun glinted off their snowy white faces so harshly that I had to squint, even behind my sunglasses. My ears began to prickle with pressure as we climbed higher, making our way towards Moose Creek. I swallowed hard and wiggled my jaw until my ears finally popped. Sweet relief.

The last time we'd packed up moving boxes and driven a U-Haul together was after college, when Kelsey and I moved to New York together. We got the smallest, cheapest truck they had because we were broke, recent graduates and had yet to accumulate many possessions. I remember blasting Britney Spears as I drove us down the Long Island Expressway and through the Queens Midtown tunnel, into the heart of Manhattan. We were ready to take on the world that day, full of hope and dreams for our future.

Now life had taken us in very different directions. I was still in New York, and still single. Kelsey was in Colorado and freshly divorced from a wealthy man almost twenty years her senior. She had a beautiful baby boy, and I had a few house-plants I was struggling to keep alive. We couldn't be in more different places in our lives, but, through all of it, our friendship never changed. I'd be there for her, no matter what, and she'd be there for me. Just the way it had always been.

The large wooden "Welcome to Moose Creek, Colorado" sign greeted us as we rode into town. I drove us down the main drag of town. It was lined with cozy coffee shops and cafes, restaurants, bars, and boutiques. A few stragglers were milling about, but since it was the middle of the day, most visitors were on the slopes and the locals were at work. It was an idyllic little town, like something you'd see in a Christmas movie. But I felt a pang of homesick-ness for the grimy streets of New York. Where were the bodegas open twenty-four hours a day? Where could I get a proper bacon, egg, and cheese? My stomach rumbled as I turned the wheel.

Kelsey's new townhouse was towards the outer edges of town, right off the main road that led up to Moose Creek Mountain, the ski resort where Kelsey would be working events. I drove up to the neat row of timber structures, their facades all evocative of a quaint log cabin. They were nestled in amongst towering pines and evergreens. It was peaceful. No wailing sirens or people yelling on the street like back home. Kelsey's new front door swung open and her mother, Dina, stood in the doorframe, Noah perched on her hip. He squealed when he saw Kelsey get out of the car.

"Hi baby boy," Kelsey trilled sweetly, as she walked up to the front door, arms outstretched to him. He leaned forward eagerly, and she scooped him up, showering his smiling face with kisses.

"How was it?" Dina asked as we followed her inside. Dina had been one of my greatest allies throughout Kelsey's relationship with Rick. We had both hoped it would be a passing phase, but he'd managed to stick around for a lot longer than either of us had wanted. Up until now.

We all settled into the new living room furniture. The three of them nestled into the navy twill sectional sofa, and I plopped down into a cozy cognac leather armchair. Even though this was definitely a downgrade for Kelsey, a home like this would be a *huge* upgrade for me. I couldn't fathom being able to even afford a pristine leather chair like this one. I tried hard not to be jealous.

"It was fine. We got the last of my stuff out." Kelsey bounced Noah on her knee as he laughed maniacally like only a baby could. I couldn't help but smile as I watched his unbridled joy.

"Well, at least that's over now," said Dina. *Understatement of the century.* Kelsey murmured in agreement. Her mother reached out a hand and lovingly tucked a stray lock of hair behind Kelsey's ear before turning her attention to me. "How long will you be in town, Annie?"

"Just a couple weeks. I've got a contract coming up that requires me to be on site with the client."

"You're a good friend for coming all the way out here to help."

I smiled at Kelsey. "I'm just lucky I'm able to, really. Perks of being a freelance graphic designer." It was cheesy, but it was true.

"Stop it! I'm the lucky one," Kelsey chimed in. I shrugged it off with a self-deprecating smile. "I mean it, Annie. I don't know what I'd do without you."

That evening, after Noah had been put down for bed, we grabbed a couple beers and got into the hot tub on the back deck. The hot water felt like a warm hug, and the steam curled the hair around my face as I piled my thick red hair into a messy bun on top of my head.

"Thanks for everything today," Kelsey reiterated in between sips of beer.

"You don't need to keep thanking me, Kels." I took a sip of beer. It felt like ice going into my veins now that I was submerged in the hot water of the jacuzzi.

Kelsey had been on a rollercoaster the past few years. And not a fun one. One of those scary, rickety, wooden ones that make you feel like you might die at any second. Against my better advice, she'd married a successful older businessman only to have it crash and burn, and her to be left standing alone on her two feet, holding a baby that Rick had little interest in, other than carrying on his family name.

Rick had swindled her good, though. Wined and dined her, whisked her away on lavish vacations, showered her with gifts. Sounds like a dream, right? Well, turns out, from every dream, you still have to wake up to reality. It had been a great way to control her and keep her hanging on, even when he'd put Kelsey at the end of his list of priorities every *other* day of the year.

Kelsey was a perfect trophy wife, in his eyes. She was beautiful, with bright blue eyes, pore-less skin, and giant, showstopping Barbie doll tits. But she was also kind, easygoing, fun, smart, and compassionate. She was *too* understanding if you ask me. That's how she ended up in this mess, after all. But she got a beautiful baby boy out of it. Noah had become the light of Kelsey's life. And she was an incredible mom—attentive, loving, patient. She'd sing to him, and his eyes would sparkle up at her. He clung to her like a baby sloth, a smile always spread across his little face.

Rick had wanted her to be a stay-at-home mom and Kelsey had obliged. But that was no longer an option without him. She'd get child support and alimony, but Kelsey didn't want to rely on that. She'd learned a big lesson from this marriage, from giving Rick everything he wanted—bending herself to his will and depending on him for money and stability. She would never make that mistake again, thank god.

"I just don't want you to feel obligated to stay here and help me. I know you have a whole life back in New York! And if you need to go home and have some downtime to yourself before that big project, I totally get it."

"I *don't* feel obligated. I want to help you."

"Okay . . . just know you can go back whenever you want to, okay?"

"I know. I only have two free weeks anyway . . ."
I nodded and took another sip of my beer, Kelsey

still eyeing me. I sighed. "Besides, this is a good distraction."

Her face softened. "Have you heard anything from *him* at all?"

Lee, the ghost of lovers' past . . . We'd been avoiding this topic all day, even though every time I glanced at my phone, I still hoped I'd see his name appear with a missed call or text. I shook my head. "No signs of life from Lee . . . he totally vanished into thin air."

"What a coward."

"Yep. And he blocked my number, my social media, everything. . . it's like he was a figment of my imagination."

"Ghosting is so cruel." Kelsey's eyes darkened with disgust. "He's a total idiot."

"I know." I groaned and picked at the label on my beer bottle. "But I'm so tired, I'm so tired of putting myself out there and dating and ghosting and . . . it's just so demoralizing. Sometimes I think I'll never find a good man."

Kelsey sighed and nodded slowly. "I know . . . I certainly don't have a great picker when it comes to men—I mean, exhibit A: Rick . . . But I have *no doubt* in my mind you will find someone who will love you and treat you right." She reached across the hot tub and gave my hand a squeeze. "I mean it."

"Thanks." I forced a small smile. I wanted to believe her. I really did. "I hope you're right . . . but for now I'm sticking to my plan. No dating, no sex, no feelings. Men are off the table for the foreseeable future."

"Amen to that." She grinned and took a sip of her beer. "You should get some skiing in while you're here . . . have some fun."

"Ugh," I groaned. "I haven't been since I was a kid. I'd totally wipe out and break something knowing me."

"Take a lesson!"

"I'm a grown-ass adult, Kels! I don't think they have ski school for adults."

"Plenty of people take ski lessons, Annie. Let me buy you some lessons, as a thank you!"

Ski lessons sounded like a miserable way to spend an afternoon to me. Kelsey looked so hopeful, but there was no way I'd put myself through that humiliation. I was not a skiing kind of girl. Athletic was *not* a word anyone had ever used to describe me.

"Please!" Kelsey's eyes were wide and excited as she smiled widely. "C'mon! There are some *really* cute ski instructors. You could do a little flirting, a little skiing?"

"No men! I told you. The last thing I want is to make a fool of myself in front of some hot dude who skis for a living."

"Oh, who cares, they're paid to teach; it's their *job*! And you can borrow one of my ski outfits. Rick spent a fortune on making sure I had the right clothes. So at least you'll look good . . . please?!"

"Ugh," I groaned. Kelsey's eyes remained pleading. "I'm sorry, but no. Not gonna happen."

Kelsey pouted and sipped her beer.

A twig suddenly snapped, puncturing our little bubble surrounding the deck. Kelsey's head swiveled around sharply, her eyes scanning the dark woods behind us. *Were we about to be in the opening of some slasher ski movie?!*

"Sorry about that, didn't mean to startle you!" I heard a male voice called out. A large shaggy dog appeared in the moonlight and ran up the deck of the townhouse next door. A man followed, emerging from the woods with an easy saunter. He was bundled up but looked to be non-threatening—average height and build, with blonde hair peeking out from under a crimson beanie. He climbed the stairs to his deck as the dog shook his coat excitedly.

"I'm Derek," he said with a wave. "And this is Coyote."

"Nice to meet you. I'm Kelsey," she said, leaning over the edge of the hot tub. Totally unperturbed that there was a strange man standing in her backyard. "I just moved in with my son Noah. And this is my friend, Annie."

"Nice to meet you both. Welcome to the neighborhood." He smiled warmly. I could only imagine he was thrilled with the new neighbor. A young, hot, single mom like Kelsey? Isn't that catnip to men?

"Thanks." Kelsey tipped her beer to him and gave him a winning smile. She was effortlessly friendly, unlike me. It took me a while to warm to strangers. I was guarded and only trusted a small group of people, especially ones that had just wandered into my best friend's yard unannounced. Kelsey, though, was charming and open. She was optimistic and believed in the best in people. We balanced each other out, I guess.

"Well, I gotta feed this one, but I'll see you around." He flashed another toothy smile in the warm glow of his deck light before sliding the glass door open and disappearing inside with Coyote.

Kelsey turned back to me, her eyebrows raised mischievously. "He's cute," she whispered.

I prickled, and Kelsey rolled her big blue eyes dramatically. "Why is he hanging out in your backyard?! Don't start hooking up with your neighbor," I warned. "That could get messy."

"No, no . . . I meant he's cute for *you*."

"God. Kels, no," I said with a forced laugh.

"What? He has a nice smile! And a cute dog."

"No dating, remember? And I'm certainly not dating some random guy that turned up in the bushes! He looks like a total snowboarder bro. '*Shred the gnar, bruh*'" I did my best stoned snowboarder dude impression.

Kelsey giggled as she sipped her beer. "Maybe that's not a bad thing! The brooding wannabe musician Brooklyn type hasn't been working for you."

"Ugh," I groaned. "That's why I'm on a dating hiatus. No musicians. No snowboarders. No men."

"Fine, fine. I won't push it, then." She smirked and drank her beer, unconvinced by my insistence.

Chapter 2

THE NEXT MORNING, I SLIPPED MY FEET INTO MY fuzzy boots and curled my fingers around a steaming mug of coffee. It was early, but I had work to do. Not bothering to zip up my puffy coat, I opened the door and began to fight with Kelsey's new garbage can. It was unwieldy and heavy, and almost as tall as me. Not that that was hard, as I barely cleared 5 feet. I began to push it down the driveway but couldn't get it to roll in a straight line. My coffee began sloshing over the side of my mug as I wrestled with the unruly receptacle.

"Shit," I muttered, trying to steer it to the edge of the driveway. My fingers began to turn blue as I gripped the garbage can in the freezing morning air. Its wheels were loud and rumbly, puncturing the otherwise quiet street.

As I struggled with my new inanimate nemesis, its weight began to take over and I felt it slipping away from me, ready to topple over. "Shit!" I yelled out—too loudly—as my mug fell to the concrete with a crash while I tried to steady the garbage can.

"Need any help?" a man's voice called out from behind me.

I swiveled around, exasperated. It was Kelsey's neighbor, the ski bro. How was he always turning up when I least expected—and least wanted to see him? His shaggy blonde hair was unbrushed and tangled. Tie-dyed sweatpants slung low across his hips, exposing the slightest sliver of skin across his abdomen.

"It's just . . . being a bit unwieldy," I croaked. "And I dropped my coffee." I nodded towards the broken ceramic mug that lay in a pile on the driveway, its contents steaming off the frozen pavement. I gripped the can tightly, doing my best to steer it, when it suddenly skidded, its bottom swinging out as it flew backwards, pushing me to the ground and flinging trash everywhere.

"Oh, for fuck's sake!" I was now splayed out on the concrete, covered in disgusting garbage, for all to see. Why couldn't I just crawl into a hole and disappear?

"Oh my god, are you okay?" He began to jog

over to me, arms outstretched. "Here, let me," he said, lifting the garbage can off me. "This thing is like half your size." I fought the urge to roll my eyes. People loved to make comments about my height. And men seemed to especially get a thrill out of pointing out my short stature. Kelsey always said they were just flirting and that men liked to feel big and strong, but *I* found it demeaning and condescending. He rolled the garbage can—with ease, of course—to the street for collection.

I brushed the trash off me, embarrassed. I'm sure my face was now a deep shade of beet red. "Thanks," I said, forcing myself to raise my eyes to him. "I'm Annie."

"Ah, yes, we met last night. I was the creep in the woods," he said with a boyish smile. As if I could forget. "I'm Derek." He reached out his hand, and I gave it a firm shake, determined to recover from my humiliation. "Are you new to Moose Creek?"

"I'm just here helping my friend out. I live in New York."

"Ah, well, this is quite a change for you, I'm sure."

"Yeah, it's pretty quiet . . . but nice." I smiled, trying to be polite. Moose Creek was charming and beautiful, yes, but I cannot imagine calling this place home. I'd be bored to tears in a matter of weeks. Where could I get a slice of pizza at 2am? Where were the art galleries or museums? I lived for the hustle and bustle of New York City. No matter the day or time, there was always something going on, something to do, people to see, places to go . . . you get the gist.

"I gotta get this cleaned up." I gestured to the pile of broken ceramic.

"Ah, get it later! Why don't you come in for a cup of coffee with me? I just turned the pot on." I paused, unsure, eyeing the mess on the driveway. "I don't bite, I promise," he added with a smile. Was this guy always so happy in the mornings?

"I really shouldn't. I smell like garbage."

"I don't care. C'mon." He motioned for me to follow him.

"Um, okay, I guess . . ."

We were greeted excitedly by his dog Coyote. Derek leaned down and gave him a good scratch behind the ears, before the dog bounded toward me. "No jumping," he warned Coyote, whose tail was wagging at a frenetic pace.

I knelt to pet him. Coyote panted happily as I scratched his scruff. He gave my nose a lick of appreciation. Despite myself, I giggled.

"Feel free to hang your coat up," Derek said, gesturing to the coat rack next to the door.

I gave Coyote a few more scratches before reluctantly rising to my feet and taking my coat off. His eyes lingered on me, hopeful for more pets.

"Um, how do you take your coffee?" he called out from the kitchen.

"Creamy, a little bit of sugar."

Clinks and clanks rattled out in a cacophony. I followed the sounds and perched against the doorframe, watching him prep the coffee. He was surprisingly meticulous as he tipped over the tiniest spoonful of sugar into what I assumed was my mug.

Derek turned around, surprised to see me spying, and handed me a stone mug. "Let me know if that tastes okay."

I brought the steaming mug up to my lips and took a slurp as delicately as I could, being careful not to burn my mouth. Surprisingly, Derek had fixed my cup of coffee exactly right. "It's perfect," I said.

"Great," he said as leaned back against the kitchen counter. "You gonna get any skiing in while you're in town?"

I shook my head. "No, not really my thing . . . I tried it once when I was a kid on a family vacation. I'm not much of an athlete."

"You don't have to be an athlete to enjoy skiing," he said with a gentle laugh. "It's beautiful, being up there on the mountain. The snow glistening in the sun. The tall pine trees towering above you. The jolt of cold air as it flies by your face . . ."

"So, you're a jock *and* a poet," I teased.

"I contain multitudes." He gave a sheepish shrug; I think trying to be cute. "And I am *not* a jock," he added emphatically.

"Hmmm," I murmured, eyeing him closely. "Hair bleached from time in the sun . . . tan, freckled skin in the middle of winter . . . broad, muscular shoulders and arms . . . you look like a jock to me."

His eyes glinted mischievously in the morning light as he gave me a wry smile. "You think my shoulders are broad and muscular?"

"As if." I laughed, a booming, full-throated laugh, and he joined in. *Was Derek flirting with me? Or, more importantly, was I flirting with him?* Suddenly, a knock rang out, rapid and frantic, pulling us out of our laughter.

"That's probably Kelsey," I said, rising from my seat to get the door. Derek followed me to the front room as I helped myself to opening the door, and sure enough, it was Kelsey, Noah bouncing on her hip in a fuzzy teddy bear onesie.

"Oh my god, I'm so glad you're here," she said. Her face was flushed from the cold and her expression a hair away from exasperation. I guess it would be one of *those* mornings. With Kelsey, I was quickly realizing that motherhood could be exhausting and that mornings were rarely slow and easy.

"Yeah, Derek invited me in for coffee. I'm sure you saw the mess I made." Kelsey looked past me at Derek, her eyebrows raised.

"Care to join?" Derek asked.

"Oh, thanks for the invite, but I have so much unpacking to get done, and Noah's hungry," she said as Noah's big blue eyes watched Coyote in wonder. "I just didn't know where Annie had gone."

"Sorry about that," I said and turned around, pressing my coffee mug into his hands. "I should get going, but thanks for the coffee, Derek. And for your help with the trashcan."

"Of course. Anytime." He flashed us a warm smile as Coyote wagged his tail behind him, watching.

"See ya," I said with a small wave.

"*He's cute, Annie*," Kelsey said in a hushed voice as we crossed his driveway and headed back to Kelsey's house. Noah babbled away on her hip incoherently, his little fuzzy feet swinging in the air.

"Sure, if you say so," I said, as noncommittally as possible.

"If *I* say so?" she asked, raising her eyebrows in disbelief. I shrugged. "Not brooding enough for you?"

"He's just not my type . . ." Historically true, but he did have a great smile. Not that I was looking for anything, I told myself. *No dating,* I repeated. *No! Men!* "I doubt I'm his type either."

"What's *that* supposed to mean? You're a total babe with a great personality and cool job." She listed these off on her fingers. "What's not to like?" I opened the front door and she and Noah glided inside. He began to squeal at a high pitch, while I tried to hide my wincing. It was way too early for that.

"Somebody's hungry . . ." Kelsey mewed into his round face. Somehow, even with the screaming, she seemed to have an infinite amount of patience for Noah. Kelsey really was so perfect it was annoying. Noah looked up at her, eyes wide. She plopped down on the sofa and pulled out her left breast. Noah immediately leaned in and began to nurse.

"Crazy to think those were the same tits you pulled out at Mardi Gras ten years ago . . ."

"Ugh, don't I know it. They're about a half a foot lower now."

"Still look good to me."

Kelsey smiled; her nose wrinkled cutely. She was effortlessly cute like that. I'd watched her move through the world, pretty and magnetic, her whole life. Things just happened to her—complementary drinks, airline upgrades, job opportunities—without her having to ask or try. And it wasn't *just* because she was a certified hottie. She was sweet and kind, radiating warmth and goodwill. There was a short period of time—adolescence mainly—that I'd envied her and this strange magnetism she seemed to possess.

Once I'd blossomed in my own way, albeit a much subtler way, I realized I in no way wanted the kind of attention she attracted. There was a darker side to it all—married men soliciting her for affairs, unwanted advances everywhere from crowded bars to business meetings, women eyeing her judgmentally solely because of her appearance. One woman once sneered at her, calling her a "bimbo" in the ugliest tone you could imagine, simply because a bartender served her first. I had to bite my tongue from unleashing my verbal wrath upon her. And of course, her jackass ex-husband—the last in the line of bad men—was the perfect example of all this. Powerful men looked at her like a prize, something to own and show off, and that never ended well.

Kelsey was a good person, a good friend. There was more to her than her beautiful—*and I mean, beautiful*—façade. "A body built for sin," is what my mother used to say shaking her head sagely, her eyes sad. I hadn't realized the implications of that when I was sixteen. Sin had sounded fun, and my breasts were still sitting at a lowly B cup compared to her Es.

Noah suckled on Kelsey as she stroked his short blonde curls with her free hand. "I think Derek was a fan of yours . . ."

"Huh?" I narrowed my eyes, skeptical.

"I *maybe* caught him checking out your ass." She grinned, enjoying this way too much.

"*Kels*, stop. No, you didn't." There was just no way. I was wearing a big coat and sweatpants, first thing in the morning. I did *not* look cute.

"Oh, I think he was enjoying the view," she teased in a fit of giggles. I covered my eyes, mildly embarrassed, but began to laugh with her. Our laughter snowballed, the hours of lost sleep from the past few days of moving compounding, until tears streamed down our faces. We were slap happy, giggling maniacally like twelve-year-olds again.

Chapter 3

"Morniiiing," Kelsey trilled as she flung my bedroom door open. "Up, up, up! I've got a surprise for you."

I squinted my eyes open groggily. "Pancakes?" I lifted my head up hopefully.

Kelsey laughed and shook her head. "There's not time for *pancakes!* I booked you a ski lesson for 10am!"

"I *told* you I didn't want that!"

"I know, I know! Don't hate me. But it'll be good for you, and you'll end up having fun."

I groaned and rolled my eyes.

"Just try it! I didn't book it to punish you," she said with a chuckle as she pulled back the curtains, letting the morning light stream in.

"If you're going to force me to take a ski lesson,

at least have the decency to make me pancakes first." I stretched my legs as far as I could and yawned, reluctantly waking my body up.

"You're right. I'll get on that." She turned on her heel and laughed to herself.

"You better!" I called after her. These better be some good pancakes if I was going to haul my ass up that mountain like a buffoon.

Luckily for Kelsey, the pancakes were delicious. And she outfitted me in a nice pair of turquoise bibs with a matching jacket. If I was about to look really dumb, at least I was gonna look *cute*. I bitched and moaned the whole way to the mountain, though, as she drove me like a mom about to drop off her insolent teenager at school. She wasn't going to get off this easily. I would take the lesson since she'd already paid, but I was not happy about it. Typical Kelsey, though, she found my petty complaining and petulance amusing. She liked to needle me, like a sister would.

At the ski school reception, I waited nervously. The jitters began to engulf me the longer I waited, as I imagined my legs dangling high above the ground helplessly on the chairlift. I wondered if I had time to throw up in the bathroom before the instructor came to collect me. And if I did vomit, would that get me out of this mess? Maybe they could even issue Kelsey a refund.

But before I could try it, the receptionist piped up. "Annie, your instructor is ready. This is Derek. Derek, this is Annie. She's a beginner."

Derek began to laugh. "Oh, I know you."

I shook my head and frowned. "No, no."

"What?" He was still laughing.

"Of *course*, you're a ski instructor."

"What's that supposed to mean?"

"I told you! You're a jock."

He gave me a wry smile and coy shrug. "C'mon. Let's get you on the slopes."

Derek took me to get my boots, skis, and poles. I awkwardly let him fit me to the right sizes and when he handed me a pair of pink sparkly children's poles, I balked.

"What? They're the right height!"

"They don't have any for adult women? Maybe sans sparkles?"

He frowned apologetically. "They're out. Busy day . . . but you can totally pull these off."

I sighed. "I guess."

This was going to be a *long* hour. Trudging alongside him outside, I felt unsteady on my feet. The boots were clunky and stiff and made me walk strangely. I was so uncomfortable; I began to dread getting on the mountain even more.

He paused and waited for me to catch up to him as my body moved jerkily. "I hate this already," I mumbled under my breath.

Derek laughed. "It'll get better once you're in the skis." He laid our skis down and offered his arm for balance as I clipped my boots into them. Even through his puffy ski jacket, I could feel that his arms were hard with muscle underneath. Derek quickly put his skis on with ease and pointed to the bunny hill. "We'll start there, okay?" He smiled reassuringly.

"Okay," I said, still hesitant.

"Move your feet like this—" he made a gliding motion. I nodded and followed suit. We glided, poles in hand, to the small bunny hill chairlift. Derek helped steer me up to the lift, where the chair scooped us up like a ladle.

"Whoa," I said, my belly flipping again. Our ski-bound legs dangled in the air as the two-seater carried us up the hill.

"You okay?" he asked, pulling the safety bar down over our laps.

"Mhmm." I nodded curtly, feeling my stomach in my throat.

"Doesn't look it . . ."

I glanced down below and immediately regretted it. My vision felt wobbly, as if I was on a ship traversing the high seas. A wave of nausea crashed over my body. I took three sharp inhales trying to calm down.

"I'm afraid of heights," I blurted out.

"Shit! Okay." His brow was furrowed in thought. "Um, this is a short lift so it will be over very soon . . . take a few deep breaths." He inhaled and nodded for me to follow along. I did. I felt my heartrate start to steady as we slowly inhaled and exhaled.

"See? We're already here." He began raising the bar. "You're going to hold your poles out, so they don't get stuck in the snow. Bend your knees a little and dismount."

"What?!"

"Let's go!" he prompted. I did as I was told and Derek gripped my elbow firmly, maneuvering me off the chairlift and out of the way. "Alright, you okay?"

"Yes, I think so." My heart was racing, so I took another deep breath.

"You got this, Annie. And I'm gonna be here the whole time."

I nodded solemnly. I would get down this tiny mountain built for children and other novices if it was the last thing I did. There was no way in hell I could ride that thing back down the other way.

"Alright. So, some basics: the best way to stop as a beginner is to pizza your skis." He demonstrated by putting the front tips of his skis together in a v-formation. I copied him. "Yep, just like that . . . I'm going to lead you down in a wide back and forth motion, like we're sweeping the side of the bunny hill. This will prevent you from gathering too much speed and getting overwhelmed, okay?"

"Okay . . ."

"And bend your knees some—like this—and don't lean forward." He made sure my form was okay, but my nerves were firing on all cylinders. I was worried I might vomit my way down the slope. "And make sure you don't cross the tips of your skis," he added. "You'll go flying." My stomach churned at the thought as my heartbeat thundered in my ears.

"You ready?"

"As ready as I'll ever be . . ." I stared down the bunny hill, my stomach feeling like it might swallow me whole.

"You got this!" Derek smiled encouragingly and motioned for me to start following him.

"Okay." I swallowed hard and began to follow him down. The cold air stung my exposed cheeks as I followed him in wide arcs down the slope, as tiny children whizzed by me. I kept my eyes trained on Derek, trying not to get distracted by these miniature intrepid skiers and snowboarders. My heart leapt into my throat as more and more of them flew past me, each one seeming to cut closer and closer to my path. I felt my legs began to wobble as one pintsized daredevil swooped in front of me.

I wailed, unable to steer out of their way. "Derek!!!" I screeched into the air like banshee as the tip of one my skis skidded over the other and I began to tumble. My legs went akimbo as my skis jettisoned themselves, landing who knows where. I'd gathered enough speed in my near collision that I began to roll like a tire down the slope. Sounds became muffled as snow filled my ears and mouth. I thought I was going to die right then and there. On the bunny hill. Death by snow. A grown woman barreling down the mountain, body surfing it like a spinning torpedo.

My momentum was suddenly halted as I peered up at Derek, mortified and dizzy. His face was a blur, but unmistakable. "Oh my god, Annie, are you okay?"

I mumbled unintelligibly, as I tried to get my bearings. "Earth . . . spinning . . ."

"Are you hurt?!" He was kneeling in front of me now.

"What?"

"Are you in pain?"

The spinning slowed down as I tried to feel my legs, my back, my arms . . . nothing felt broken now, but I knew I'd be sore tonight.

"I don't think so," I said, as I began to look around. I had managed to roll my way down to nearly the bottom of the bunny hill. A gaggle of children had paused to watch me, mouths agape. Some were even giggling. I wanted to crawl into a cave and die, alone with what shred of dignity I may have left. My cheeks went hot as more people began to gather, watching curiously. Who was this giant child that had just rolled down the mountain? Oh, it wasn't a child? A thirty-year-old woman with zero coordination and skill?

"I'm never doing this again," I said in a low harsh voice, practically growling.

"Annie . . . I'm sorry, this was just like a freak accident!"

"No!" I fumbled getting to my feet.

"Please! One more run. If you leave it now, it will only be scarier to try again next time." Derek looked at me pleadingly, his goggles atop his beanie.

His eyes were wide and full of concern, his cheeks rosy and wind chapped.

"Next time?! There won't be a next time! I'm done," I huffed. I don't know where my skis had landed, and I didn't care. I hobbled in my boots to the rental area, seething, and practically threw them on the counter as I made my way out of the lodge.

When Kelsey finally came to pick me up, I burst into tears. "It was horrible!"

"Oh Annie, I'm so sorry . . . I really thought you'd have fun."

"Well, I didn't! It was awful!" I heaved thick sobs as Kelsey kept glancing at me with pity as she drove us home.

"What happened?" she asked quietly. I could tell she was using her mom voice on me.

I gave her the play by play of the lesson through sniffles. And I didn't bother sparing any of the humiliating details.

"Oh Annie . . ." was all Kelsey managed to say.

When we got home, she drew me a bath and made me soup while Dina cared for Noah. I knew I was being a giant baby, but the embarrassment of the morning was too much to bear. Maybe I should have kept at it, maybe the storming off made everything worse . . . but I'd been pushed to my breaking point. I had never wanted to ski in the first place, and now I'd been proven right. I never should have even tried. I promised to myself that I would never, ever trying skiing again. No matter who forced me up that mountain.

That night, I was sulking in bed, doodling in my sketch pad—lots of sad, spindly trees—when a knock at the door downstairs rang out. I heard Kelsey open it and Derek's voice, muffled, ask how I was doing. I couldn't make out what else they said, but I was glad she didn't make me come downstairs to see him. She knew me better than that.

Chapter 4

I SAT NEXT TO THE BABY MONITOR AS NOAH NAPPED upstairs. I had to mockup some logos for a new client and was trying to find whatever free time to work on it that I could. I was on baby duty since Kelsey had to go up the mountain for orientation. She seemed excited and nervous to have her old job back. It had been a good five years since she'd worked there, and the resort was more popular than ever before.

Moose Creek was still more quaint and accessible than Aspen or Park City, but it was no longer a hidden gem. It was quickly growing into a popular skiing and snowboarding destination for the millennial set. They even had a Michelin starred restaurant now.

Rick had taken us there the last time I visited

them at their old house—a mere three months before they called it quits. He wined and dined us proudly but kept getting up to take work calls.

"Sorry about that," Kelsey had said, visibly annoyed.

Noah was only a couple months old at that point. He was home with their nanny—Rick insisted Kelsey be a stay-at-home mom but *also* have fulltime help so she wouldn't get too rundown. Really, he just wanted her body to bounce back as soon as biologically possible and she needed time and sleep and a personal trainer for that. A nanny ensured she'd be able to devote time to getting her back to the old Kelsey. *Gross.*

"It's fine, Kels." I had tried to give her a reassuring smile, but she remained miffed.

"No, it's incredibly rude. And he's always on his phone. When he's even around."

"I know things have been hard—"

"Hard is an *understatement*, Annie. He's usually at the house in the city—'for work'—" she mimed quotation marks, "but I think he's having an affair." She didn't even look sad or hurt. Just angry and resentful, her face dripping with disdain.

Turns out, of course, Kelsey had been right. Although it wasn't just *one* singular affair. Turns out, Rick had two different girlfriends. One in San Francisco and another in Hong Kong. He'd snagged the best woman in the entire world—*okay, sure, I was biased, but still*—and that wasn't enough to satisfy him. He was a real piece of shit.

Back in Kelsey's new Rick-free townhouse, I checked the baby monitor again—the tiny black and white video showed Noah sleeping soundly in his crib—as I wrapped a faux-fur throw blanket around me. It was *so* cold here. I thought New York suffered some cold winters, but these mountains felt practically arctic. I eyed the fireplace on the other side of the room—a real wood burning fireplace and one of the major selling points for Kelsey—and padded over to it.

I held the blanket around me tight and stared down at the fireplace. *How does one build a fire?* I don't think we even had any wood to burn . . . but now that I had it stuck in my head that I could have a delightful, cozy crackling fire to work by, I had to make it happen. And thankfully, I'd seen a huge stack of firewood next to Derek's front door. I just needed to covertly grab a few logs, so I could avoid having to face him after yesterday's ski debacle.

I grabbed the baby monitor and slipped on my snow boots, ditching the blanket for my puffer coat. Keeping one eye on the screen showing sleeping Noah the entire time, I quickly ran next door.

Hopefully, he was on the mountain working and not home. I quietly took the first log atop the pile when Coyote began barking on the other side of his door. Shit. *Please don't be home. Please don't be home.* I quickly piled two more logs into my arms and turned around, ready to make a run for it.

"Hey!"

I spun around, eyes wide. "Hi, Derek."

"Whatchya doin' there?" He smirked, bemused, and pointed at the firewood I was trying to abscond with.

My cheeks flushed. "Um . . . I wanted to build a fire, but we don't have any wood?" It came out like a question, as if I was unsure of what I'd been trying to do.

"And you didn't want to ask? Gotta say, I didn't peg you as a thief," he teased, his lips curling into a smile.

"I didn't think you were home?" Again, I was evasive, speaking only in questions.

"Wouldn't hurt to knock and check, though, right?" It was obvious Derek was enjoying this, making me squirm.

I laughed awkwardly. "I guess not . . ." He continued to eye me, his eyes dancing with amusement. I sighed, relenting. "I didn't want to see you after yesterday."

"You know, I came by last night to check on you."

"I heard."

He sighed, his smile turning sincere. "I'm really sorry about everything. I feel awful that you took such a bad spill."

"Wasn't your fault . . . Everybody should have just listened to me, though. I am *not* meant to ski."

"Ah, falling your first time is a right of passage!"

I stared at him blankly. The way Derek said 'first time' implied there would be a 'second time.'

"Just trying to make you feel better."

"Most people probably don't roll down the bunny hill to an audience of amused children."

He chuckled. "No, that was the first time I'd witnessed that in my career."

I shifted my weight, still feeling awkward as hell. He took a step closer. God, his eyes were *really* blue in the afternoon light, like a forget-me-not in June.

"Did you get enough?" He gestured to the three logs I'd grabbed.

"Um, maybe?"

He began to laugh. "You don't know how to build a fire, do you?"

"I do not."

"Lucky for you, I'm an expert fire builder." Derek pushed his sleeves up to his elbows, revealing taut forearms, and began to gather the chopped wood. I couldn't let my eyes linger for too long on them without feeling an unwelcome stirring at the bottom of my stomach.

He was just so . . . manly? Yes, *manly*. And I was used to pale, lanky, sad boys who were trying to be the next John Mayer—gross, I know, but guilty as charged. I had a type. And Derek was most certainly *not* that type. Derek looked like the kind of guy who would look right through me, as if I wasn't even standing in front of him. So why couldn't I pry my eyes away from his muscly forearms tensing as he stacked the firewood higher and higher against them. Plus, he was Kelsey's neighbor, and I had no business in making her new living situation awkward for her. I didn't even live in this state!

"You okay?" His brows were furrowed as he eyed me, his arms steadying the towering stack of wood.

"Oh yeah, sorry . . ." I let out a soft, awkward laugh. "My brain just went . . . elsewhere." I led him across the drive and back into Kelsey's house. Glancing at the baby monitor still in hand, I could see that Noah was still in angel baby mode, sleeping soundly. I pressed my ear to the speaker and double checked—yep, there were little heavy breaths echoing in his room.

Derek set down the stack of firewood next to the brick hearth. "Alright, first we have to open the flue damper," he said, sliding his hand along the top frame of the fireplace until he found the lever. He pulled it open. "Don't want to smoke your place out."

"Right," I said, following along.

"Then you wanna grab your smaller logs—like these—" he held up a couple slender pieces of wood "—and put those in first." He set them inside the grate, then turned around to face me. "Do you have any newspaper?"

"Huh?"

"For kindling."

"Um, I don't think so? I mean, she just moved in, but let me go see what I can find." I padded into the kitchen and scanned the countertops. They were clear, except for a few cereal boxes and Kelsey's breast pump drying on a small tea towel. "I don't see anything," I said as I walked back into the room.

Derek was already on his feet, heading towards the door. "I'll go grab some at my place." He hurried out and a few minutes later, reappeared with a copy of Sunday's New York Times.

"You get the New York Times? In actual, old-fashioned, newsprint?"

"Yeah," he said with a pleased smile. "But just the Sunday edition. I like the crossword."

"Wow." Maybe he wasn't such a stereotypical jock after all. I didn't even get a hard copy of the New York Times. And I *lived* in New York.

"Remember? I contain multitudes," he added, taking notice of my surprised face.

"Clearly. A mountain man that can build a fire, ski a black diamond, *and* reads the Times?" He smiled at me, and I noticed that he had two sweet dimples form when his lips curled just the right way.

"Well, now that we have the kindling," he said, breaking eye contact and turning back to the fireplace. "We can crumple it up, toss it in, and put the bigger logs in there." He nestled each piece of the puzzle in the grate before pulling out a lighter from his back pocket.

"And now we light it." Reaching his arm in carefully, he flicked the lighter on and held it to a piece of newspaper. It caught flame and began to swell, slowly enveloping the kindling and surrounding logs. Derek stepped back and stood beside me as we watched the fire grow until it was a beautiful, roaring fire, the flames crackling like a megaphone held to a bowl of Rice Krispies.

"Good work," I murmured, my eyes mesmerized by the blaze. "You weren't kidding about being an expert fire builder." I glanced at the baby monitor again, making sure Noah was still asleep—and he was. I swiveled to face Derek. "Thanks for your help. I owe you a drink or something." *Dammit, did I really just say that?* I hoped he didn't think I was hitting on him.

"Ah, it's no big deal. I'm happy to help." He was going to brush aside my offer—thank god. He was keeping it casual and neighborly.

But just as I thought he was about to head for the door, he narrowed his eyes and smirked. "But I'll still take you up on that drink sometime."

"Really?" I tried to hide my surprise. It wasn't like I was disappointed . . . just hadn't expected that.

"Yes, really," Derek said with a laugh.

"Okay, well whenever you're free then. We'll get you that drink."

"Tomorrow night? I can give you a proper introduction to Moose Creek."

"Uh, yeah, let me just double check with Kelsey tonight but that should work."

"Great. And now I'll get another chance to try and convince you to go skiing again." He gave me a wink as he headed out the door.

I rolled my eyes. *No chance in hell.* "Alright then," I said, leaning against the doorframe.

"I'll get you on those slopes if it's the last thing I do, Annie!" His face spread into a wide cocky smile as he crossed the driveway.

"Yeah, yeah, yeah . . ." I called after him. *We'll see about that, Derek.*

THAT NIGHT KELSEY AND I SAT AROUND HER kitchen table, having a glass of wine, and debriefing about our days after she'd put Noah to bed.

Her first day back on the job after such a long hiatus had gone well enough, and she was in good spirits. "You know, they're having their first film festival here in a month."

"Really?"

"Yeah, Sundance and Telluride already do their own. Some actor who has a house here decided he wanted to partner with the resort and start his own festival."

"That's awesome. Are you going to have to do a lot of work for that?"

"I think so . . . they didn't tell me too much about it today because I think they were worried they were going to overwhelm me."

"Are you nervous?"

"Eh, I don't know . . . I think I'm just taking it all in. I want to do a good job—it's just changed a lot since I worked there five years ago. Moose Creek has become so much more of a *destination*, rather than a hidden gem for ski bums in the know."

"I'm sure they understand, and I'm *also* sure that you're going to do a *great* job. You are an incredible and meticulous planner and party host!"

"That's true—can't argue with that," Kelsey said with a pleased little sigh. "But enough about me, Annie! How's work going for you? Is it tough being here at all, away from your usual routine?"

"Not really. My work is so solitary and luckily, I'm good about keeping boundaries with my clients. I do my doodles and designs, and they're usually pretty pleased."

"As they should be. They're more than doodles and designs. You're good at what you do."

"Mhmm," I murmured, nodding. "Sooo . . . Derek came over to help me with the fireplace this afternoon."

Kelsey squealed with delight. "Ooooh, that's so cute. Like something out of a Hallmark movie."

"Oh, it was *very* mountain man builds fire for clueless city girl . . . and he kind of asked me to get a drink with him tomorrow night."

"A date?! *Annie!* That's so exciting!" Kelsey looked at me, her big blue eyes wide and sparkling.

"No, no, *not* a date! Definitely not a date . . . I just said I owed him a drink for his help."

"And how do you know it's *not* a date?"

"I could tell . . . it's not. He just wants to convince me to try skiing again, I think," I said with a shrug.

Kelsey's blue eyes narrowed at me, doubtful. I'm sure if Derek had asked *her* out for a drink, it would be with romantic intentions, but not with me. There was no way. He was classically handsome and fit, and outdoorsy with a laidback attitude. I could be goofy, verging on awkward, and liked to draw and knit—both very much indoor activities that didn't require any semblance of athleticism. The only marathon I'd ever be doing was of reality TV.

"Besides, there's no way a guy like him would be into a girl like me. We are way too different," I added.

"*Annie*," Kelsey balked.

"Yes, I'm amazing, I know," I said with a little laugh. "But that doesn't mean I'm his cup of tea or he's even mine."

"I knew it, not nearly sad and selfish enough for you."

"Ouch."

"Hey, you know you have bad taste in men, historically." And I did. They would all fall under the category of hipster fuckboys. Guys who were artsy and funny and good in bed. They flirted and bantered and made you feel special, only to leave within a few months. Everything was on their timeline, their schedule. I had never been a priority in any of their lives.

"I know." I sighed, nodding. "But seriously, this drink is just a friendly gesture. It's not a big deal."

"Okay," Kelsey relented with a shrug before taking a long sip of wine. But I could tell she didn't believe me one bit.

Chapter 5

THE DOORBELL RANG OUT AND I JUMPED UP FROM the couch to get the door. Derek was going to drive us to a local watering hole, and I'd been ready and waiting for fifteen minutes. I was *always* ready for things early. *Warning signs of a neurotic single New Yorker,* I thought to myself.

"Hi," I said, trying to sound upbeat, as I swung the door open.

Derek stood bundled up on the doorstep and waved a mittened hand. "Hey, ready to rock and roll?"

I laughed.

"What?" he asked, cocking his head to the side.

"'*Ready to rock and roll?*' Such a dad thing to say," I teased.

He shrugged and smiled as he led me to his car,

a Jeep. *Typical.* Derek jogged ahead of me and opened the passenger door like a gentleman.

"Oh wow, great service," I said. "I'll be sure to leave a five-star review." I climbed inside. He'd left the car running so it was toasty and warm, which was surprisingly thoughtful.

Derek chuckled as he ran to his side of the car and hopped in. The snow-covered evergreens towered like dark angels over the road as he drove us into town.

"You know, I don't think I've been picked up and driven somewhere like this since high school," I mused as the moonlight shimmered on the snowbanks.

"Really?"

"Yeah . . . I mean I've lived in the city my whole adult life, so I take the subway or taxis everywhere."

"Well, a good Colorado boy picks his date up and drops her off. Door-to-door service, little lady," he said with a playful imitation twang. Ugh. Did he just say *date*?

"Was that your version of a southern accent?"

"It was, yes ma'am."

"I think you should stick to skiing. It sounded vaguely Irish," I laughed.

"Can you do any better?" He raised an eyebrow, as if to challenge me.

"No. I definitely cannot. And I won't even try and offend the good people of the South."

He smiled at me, another boyish grin, which I was beginning to realize must be a signature of his. "So, you're about to get the *real* Moose Creek experience. Nell's Tavern is a local's spot, and it's very special to me."

"Ah, is that what you tell *all* the girls?"

"Oh yeah, it's my go-to move. Is it working?"

I let out a laugh as I side-eyed him.

"But actually, *no*, I have never brought a woman here." *Not a date spot then, phew.* Derek parked the car in front of the tavern, and I followed him inside.

A voice called out his name as he opened the door. "Derek!" The woman behind the bar waved and made her way toward us. She had silver-streaked hair in a long braid that cascaded down her back and wore worn-out denim overalls. Her wrinkled hands were adorned with turquoise rings. Nell had the effortlessly cool, laidback aura of a woman who'd lived her life on the slopes.

"Hey, Nell," Derek said, his arms outstretched to hug her. I guess this was *the* eponymous Nell. "This is Annie," he added as they hugged.

"Hi," I said with a smile.

"*Annie*," Nell repeated as she reached out and

gave me a very firm handshake. "Lovely to meet you, and welcome. What can I get you two?"

Derek turned to me. "What are you feeling?"

I scanned the taps. But who was I kidding? I didn't know enough about beer to make a judgment call. "I'll take whatever lager you recommend, Nell." I knew I liked lagers fine enough and that was about the extent of my beer knowledge. I preferred to drink a good stiff dirty martini or glass of wine, but Nell's Tavern didn't strike me as the sort of place you ordered a Sancerre.

"Make that a pitcher," Derek added. He was clearly the all-American, beer-drinking type.

Nell slid the overflowing pitcher across the bar, and Derek carefully carried it to a worn booth hugging the wall. I unzipped my coat and slid across the bench, settling into the seat as Derek poured us each a beer.

"So, this is authentic Moose Creek . . ." I said as I swiveled my head around, scanning the bar. There were two pool tables in the back with a cluster of people gathered around them. Old-school vinyl booths lined the walls, several of them full. Some patrons were eating, others just drinking. A jukebox sat in the corner. Two skinny, hipster-looking dudes were flipping through its options. Vintage neon signs washed the room in a warm glow. It felt a bit timeless, like I wasn't sure which decade we were in. It wasn't the kind of place I'd find in the city, but it was charming, even if the floors seemed a bit sticky and the vinyl on the booths was beginning to fray.

"Yep." He held up his beer. "Cheers."

I raised my glass to meet his. "Cheers." The foam tickled my upper lip as I took a long sip. "How long have you lived in Moose Creek?"

"A long time . . . a decade, I think? I moved out here after college."

"Wow, you must have really seen it change then. I know Kelsey talks about how it's become a lot more popular."

"Yeah, it's a different town now than it used to be. It's always been a great little ski town, but it felt like nobody outside of Colorado knew about it until a few years ago. That's when I really noticed a lot more *actual* tourists."

"Do you miss how it used to be?"

"Honestly, not really. I make a lot more money now with the influx of visitors. Demand for ski lessons just keeps going up. I like that other people love Moose Creek now too. It's not just for me." He took a pleased swig of his beer. "What about you? How long have you lived in New York City?"

"About eight years . . . have you ever been?"

He nodded. "Once—when I was twelve. We

went there on a family vacation. I had never seen that many buildings before, or that many people in one place. It was crazy." He laughed, his eyes crinkling warmly. "Do you ever get used to it?"

"To there being people everywhere?"

"Yeah."

"I guess so." I gave a little shrug. "I like that there are always people around, though."

"Really?"

"Yeah, you're never really alone. I mean, you are, but it's so anonymous. Like I can go to dinner or a movie by myself and it's perfectly normal. Nobody looks at you strangely or cares. It's liberating."

"Huh, guess I never really thought about it like that." He took a long sip of his beer as an awkward silence began to stretch between us. Thankfully, Nell saved the day. She suddenly appeared next to the booth holding a platter of chicken tenders. "Figured you'd want your favorite," she said to Derek with a knowing smile as she set it down on the table.

"Aw, thanks, Nell. You're the best," he said.

"I know," she said with a wink.

"You new to town, Annie? Or just on vacation?" she asked, turning her attention to me.

"Oh, I'm here helping my friend through a tough time."

"That's a good friend," Nell said as she nodded approvingly. "How long you in town then?"

I fought the urge to laugh. I felt I was suddenly in a game of twenty questions. "About a week and a half left, then I have to head back home for work."

"Which would be? What do you do for work?"

Derek began to laugh. "Okay, okay, Nell, this isn't a job interview."

"What?! I can ask whatever I want to. She's in *my* bar."

I stifled my laughter. "I'm a graphic designer."

"Are we good here?" Derek asked. He had his wallet pulled out to pay. It was the most un-laidback I'd seen him thus far, and I found it *very* amusing.

Nell rolled her eyes. "Yes, we're good here . . . so touchy today, my, my, my . . ." she said, shaking her head as she smirked playfully. "Well, it was lovely to meet you, Annie. Hope you enjoy the tenders."

"Thank you, Nell. Likewise," I said with a nod. She smiled and headed back to the bar. "These look good," I mused, scanning the hot pile of fried chicken tenders.

"They're delicious. But you *have* to eat them with the homemade ranch." He picked up the ramekin of creamy ranch and demonstrated by dipping a tender in it, as if he was a spokesperson on an infomercial.

"Ah, yes, I see," I said with a chuckle. But I followed suit and was quickly nodding enthusiastically. "Okay, *yes*, that is delicious. What is in that ranch? It's fucking amazing."

"No idea. It's a secret recipe. I've tried plenty of times to wrangle it out of Nell and Rita. Neither of them will give it away."

"Who's Rita?"

"Oh, that's Nell's partner. They run it together. . . Do you have a boyfriend back in New York?"

I laughed and shook my head vigorously. "Nope. Definitely not."

"Sounds like there's more to that story . . ." He smirked, looking cute as he raised his eyebrows.

"I got ghosted a few weeks ago. By a guy I dated for five months."

Derek's mouth fell open. "No way."

"Yep. It's, unfortunately, pretty on brand for me."

"That's awful, I'm sorry. What an asshole." He shook his head and rubbed his jaw thoughtfully. "Damn."

I wanted to laugh at his reaction. He was *so* earnest, it almost hurt. "It happens." I shrugged, trying to be casual. He didn't need to know how cut up I was about Lee. And that I'd spent the first week of radio silence from him in utter agony, listening to his favorite Morrissey (because, of course) song on Spotify. I barely slept and couldn't eat anything but saltines, I was so anxious. Derek definitely didn't need to know how pathetic I could be.

"It shouldn't," he insisted.

"Ok, so do *you* have a girlfriend?"

"No . . . I've been living the single ski bum life for a couple years."

"Ah, that tracks," I teased. "No woman can compete with the thrill of the slopes, I guess." I was surprised by the hint of defensiveness I could hear in my voice. Why did I care if Derek wasn't the kind of guy who wanted a girlfriend?

He laughed, shrugging playfully. "Skiing is my life, what can I say?"

"And what is it about skiing that made you decide to dedicate your life to it?"

"It's the best feeling in the world, flying down the mountain, the wind ripping through you . . . the fresh air and great outdoors can't be beat, either." He paused, scratching his eyebrow in thought. "Skiing is both peaceful and exhilarating. There aren't many things on earth that give you that combo . . . So, what do I have to do to get you back up on that mountain?" Derek looked at me intently, a sly smile spreading across his face slowly.

"Ugh . . ." I groaned. "I'd rather spend the day at the DMV than try skiing again. And that place is hell on earth."

Derek snorted. "C'mon . . . please?" He widened his eyes and pouted his lips playfully. "Please?"

"Why is it *so* important that I go skiing?"

"Because it's the best feeling in the world and I'm determined to make you see that. It's my duty and moral obligation as a Moose Creek Mountain ski instructor."

I laughed. "Good luck with that."

"One lesson. You don't even have to pay. Just let me try?" He looked so determined as he ran his hands through his shaggy blonde hair, his eyes fixed on me.

"I don't know . . ."

"Just one. What are you so afraid of?"

"Are you serious? Did you not witness my utterly humiliating and public wipe out?"

He nodded, a conspiratorial glint in his eyes. "I did, but the law of probability dictates that you won't fall like that again."

"Oh, now you're a statistician?"

"Come on, Annie. Just give me one more

chance?" He searched my face hopefully, and dammit, if he wasn't cute doing it.

My eyes narrowed, and I let out an exasperated gasp. "*Fine*. One more lesson."

"Yes, thank you!" He took a defiant sip of his beer. "You're going to love it, I promise." Another boyish grin. I was now certain he had to know the kind of power that smile could wield.

"Don't make promises you can't keep, Derek," I said in a sing-song voice.

"Oh, I'd never," he said with an arch of his brow.

"Oh my god, Derek?!" a voice trilled out from across the room. I spun my head around to see a tall woman with sleek black hair and stiletto boots sashaying towards our booth. A group of women similarly overdressed were huddled by the bar.

"Nina? What are you doing here?" Derek asked, his lips now a tight smile. The boyish grin had totally disappeared.

"Oh, just grabbing drinks out on our last night in town . . ." She glanced at me, her heavily mascaraed eyes narrowing.

"This is my friend Annie," Derek said, his voice tinged with apprehension. He glanced at me apologetically. *Was this an ex-girlfriend?*

"Hi," she said curtly before refocusing on

Derek. "Are you around later? I'd love to see you one more time before I leave . . ." She smiled coyly as she subtly leaned her chest down, so he could get a better view of the cleavage peeking out from her low-cut sweater.

Derek shifted in his seat. "Um, I've got an early start in the morning."

"It's my last night!" Nina whined as she pouted her heavily lacquered lips.

"I'm sorry. I can't tonight . . . but it was great teaching you. And you had some incredible runs!" he added brightly.

She sighed, frustrated. "Yeah. Well, maybe I'll see you next year." She turned on her heel and marched back to her friends before Derek could even say goodbye.

"Sorry about that . . ." he said awkwardly. "She took lessons with me this week."

"*Just* lessons?" I teased, trying not to laugh too loudly. Now was not the time for my usual unbridled cackle.

"Yeah, we may have had a . . . night together." Of course, they did. I had pegged him right after all. And while I love to be proven right, thinking about him rolling around in bed with Nina stung a little. Why did I care? *Remember, Annie, absolutely no dating.*

He sighed and ran his fingers through his mop of hair. "A lot of these women come out here on vacation, wanting to have a bit of fun . . . a little escape from their lives and routines back home . . ."

"And they just throw themselves at you?"

"Hey, your words, not mine."

I snickered. He smiled and shrugged, feigning guilt.

"Will you still take a lesson with me?"

"Ugh. Yeah, I guess," I said, sighing. "Just don't expect me to seduce you like Nina."

He laughed. "I'd never . . ."

"Good."

THE NEXT MORNING, KELSEY WAS ALREADY AWAKE and eating breakfast in the kitchen when I woke up. I could hear the coffee maker gurgling and her shuffling around while Noah squealed at random intervals. I padded downstairs and walked into the kitchen.

"Hiiiii," I trilled in a high whisper.

Kelsey spun around. "Tell me everything!"

Noah was sitting in his highchair and began slamming his tiny little hands down on the tray, excited to see me. I walked over to him and kissed his sweet little head. "Morning, Mr. Baby."

"Don't get distracted by his cuteness—I need to know the dirty details about your date!" She grabbed two mugs from the cabinet and fixed our coffees, keeping one eye on my expectantly the entire time.

"It wasn't a date!" I insisted. *Why did I have to keep telling her this? . . . And more importantly, why did I have to keep telling myself?*

"Fine, how was your not-a-date-date?" She handed me my mug and I took a long slow sip, being careful not to burn my mouth. "Where did you go?"

"We went to Nell's Tavern."

"Nell's? Okay, so he was showing you some local flavor. Cute."

"Yeah, apparently it's his favorite bar. He's tight with Nell."

"Everybody loves her. But god, I haven't been to Nell's in ages. It wasn't Rick's style." Figures. Not enough top shelf Scotch to throw money at probably. She poured some Cheerios onto Noah's highchair tray and then sat down at the table. "Did he at least manage to convince you to give skiing another try?"

"Ugh," I groaned. "He did. I caved. I promised him one lesson, and that's it."

"Good," Kelsey said with an approving smile.

"But I'm not going to like it."

"Yeah, yeah," she said with an eye roll. "Well, I've gotta get ready and head to work. Mom should be here soon to take care of Noah so you can focus on your work."

"Great. Are you excited for your second day?"

"Yes! That actor who founded the film festival will be coming in. Everybody is *very* excited."

"Sounds like it's gonna be a really cool job."

"I think so." She nodded and smiled before heading upstairs. I sipped my coffee peacefully and watched Noah play with his cheerios, eating one piece for every one he threw to the ground.

Chapter 6

"PLEASE BE MY DATE TONIGHT. I KNOW IT'S LAST minute, but it will be fun, I promise!" Kelsey looked at me, her blue eyes wide and hopeful. "Pleeease!" She'd found out about a last-minute work party to celebrate the fancy Hollywood actor's arrival and didn't want to fly solo yet, as she still didn't know many of her coworkers.

"Ughhhh," I groaned playfully. "Fine, you know I can't say no to you."

"I know," she said smugly. "Mom, do you mind staying longer and watching Noah?"

"Of course not," Dina said, Noah still in her arms. Dina loved being a grandmother and doting on her grandson. She barely ever put him down; she'd carry him around the house, quietly narrating life to him for as long as he'd let her. "It'll be good for you to go out and have some fun."

"And who is this guy again?" I asked.

"Cash Taylor, the star of the *Never Die* movies. Rick was a big fan." Kelsey smirked. I knew she'd be excited to hold that over his head at some point.

"Ah, okay. I don't think I've ever seen any of those . . . they're superhero movies?"

"No! Spy movies. And he's *very* sexy in them."

"Okay . . ." I had no idea who she was talking about.

Kelsey shook head and pulled out her phone. She googled him and pulled up some red-carpet photographs. He was tall, dark, and handsome with a true Hollywood megawatt smile. "See?"

"Ah, okay, I've definitely seen that guy before."

"Duh, everyone has!" Kelsey looked at me, brimming over with excitement. "Well, he's going to be there tonight, so just be cool, okay?"

"I don't think I'm the one who has to worry about being cool around Mr. Hollywood," I teased. Kelsey's face flushed adorably. She rarely got worked up over men.

"It's just that my job is riding on this!" she insisted. "It has nothing to do with the fact that he is famous . . . or incredibly gorgeous and sexy . . . and smells really good."

"Oh, so you've smelled him?!"

"Maybe . . ." Kelsey smirked.

"So, how dressed up do I have to get for this party?"

Kelsey paused; lips pursed in thought. "I'd go with like a cute sweater dress and over the knee boots, or maybe a sexy blazer over faux leather leggings."

"Yeah, Kels, I don't have any of that."

"You can borrow mine!"

"I don't know if I could pull off either of those looks . . ." I furrowed my brow doubtfully.

"Of course, you can! You're a total babe, Annie. You could wear anything and look amazing."

I laughed at her unwavering positivity.

"I mean it!"

"Fine, fine . . . no leather pants though. I draw the line at that. I've seen *Friends*."

Kelsey snorted. "Sweater dress it is. And you're lucky we're the same shoe size too." I don't know if I would call that lucky, as I was slightly dreading having to wear over-the-knee boots. I was a sexual creature, sure, but I had never felt comfortable in clothing that screamed *sexy* the way Kelsey did. And over-the-knee boots fell into that category in my mind.

I followed her up to her bedroom and she

opened her closet door, thoughtfully examining its contents. It was about a quarter of the size of her old walk-in closet—and stuffed to the brim. Rick had loved to take Kelsey shopping and dress her up like his own personal Barbie doll. And Kelsey enjoyed it too. Clothes had always looked beautiful and effortless on her. No awkward clinging or gaping that seemed to happen so often on me. I was short, so tops were always too long, the armpits hitting me at strange places. And my butt was big for my stature so finding pants and jeans were a nightmare. There would inevitably be a huge gaping at the waist just to get something that could fit my generous behind and thighs.

Kelsey thumbed through her selection of sweater dresses that were draped over thin velvet hangers and pulled out a dark olive green one with a drapey cowl neck. "This is your color," she said, holding it up to me. "Put it on."

I stripped down to my underwear and tugged the dress over my head before checking myself out in her gilded full-length mirror.

"Looks great on you," said Kelsey.

"For once, I actually agree with you." I twisted my body and examined myself from different angles. It was a *yes*. The green made my red hair pop and my brown eyes sparkle, and it draped beautifully across my body.

"Now try it with these." Kelsey handed me a pair of charcoal suede high-heel over-the-knee boots. I eyed them, dubious. "Do it," she insisted. She didn't joke around when it came to fashion.

I pulled them on, gently working the stretchy suede up over my calves and knees. They felt expensive—I bet Rick had spent a fortune on them. Once they were fully on, I stood up, three inches taller but still a good head shorter than Kelsey. She nodded approvingly.

I looked at myself in the mirror. I'd never worn anything like this outfit, but I looked good—sexy without trying too hard. It was that effortlessness that Kelsey oozed. She'd somehow picked out the perfect pieces to give me that same air. "Damn," I murmured. Kelsey chuckled softly, pleased with herself. "Thanks, Kels."

"I *knew* you'd look hot in that . . . wear it with your gold hoops."

"Yes, ma'am," I said with the seriousness of a soldier before marching into the guest room and slipping my trusty pair of slender gold hoops through my earlobes. My mom had given them to me for my twenty-first birthday, and I still treasured them ten years later.

I headed back into Kelsey's room, where she was struggling to coax her pleather leggings on. "Fuuuuuck," she grunted, frustrated. I let out a big laugh. She looked ridiculous, squirming all over the bed, legs flailing.

"And that's why I gave a hard no to those."

"But they look sooooo good on me," she whined.

"*Everything* looks good on you, Kels!"

A slew of expletives and angry mutterings escaped her lips as she continued to writhe on the bed, fighting with the leggings. She'd managed to get them mid-thigh at least.

"Is it really worth this?" I watched her, bemused.

"Yes!" she cried out, exasperated. "Now come here and help me get them over my ass."

I crawled onto the bed as she rolled onto her belly. I gave the waist band a good strong tug, yanking them up forcefully over her perfectly sculpted bum. She let out a sigh of relief. "Better now?" I asked.

"Yes. Much better," she said with a pleased sigh. "Thanks." She got up and looked in the mirror, a smile spread wide across her face. "Perfect," she murmured.

She padded over to the closet and selected a

slim fitting black blazer with a plunging neckline. Gingerly, she threaded her arms through the sleeves. She looked so chic. "I think this looks good without being too intimidating, right?"

"Yes," I said, nodding approvingly. "You look great, Kels."

She let out a hesitant sigh and sat on the edge of the bed. "I'm actually . . . a little nervous."

"Yeah?" I prompted, sitting down next to her. Kelsey was *never* nervous.

"Yeah." She turned to face me, folding her legs up in front of her, the pleather squeaking. "The resort has changed a lot since I last worked there . . . this job is so much *bigger* now. It used to just be helping to plan weddings and family reunions . . . now it's an entire film festival. And I don't know anything about film!"

"Well, that's where Cash and his team come in, right? They don't expect you to be a film expert. Plus, you've seen all of *his* films." I gave her shoulder a reassuring squeeze. "You got your job back because you're good at event planning and you're fun to work with—don't forget that!"

"Ugh," she groaned. "I know, I know . . . but I feel so rusty." She bit her lip and paused; her brow knitted together. I hated seeing Kelsey feel so insecure; it felt like it went against the natural order of things. "And now there's a whole new events team to work with, and I feel like they're judging me."

"For what?!"

"For having taken a five-year break from working and basically being a trophy wife . . . I could tell the minute they met me that they thought I was an underqualified idiot. *Oh, here comes the blonde bimbo with big tits and too much makeup on, wearing heels to a ski resort, like a moron.*"

"Kelsey! No way! I'm sure they don't think that."

"You should have seen the way they looked at me, Annie."

"Well, if that's what they were *really* thinking, you'll just have to prove them wrong."

"I know," she said, resolutely. "Story of my life." Kelsey was used to people making assumptions about her because of her appearance. It was easier for some to write her off as a beautiful idiot than face their own jealousy and internalized misogyny, I'd guess.

"They sound boring and ugly and rude," I said playfully, nudging her with my elbow.

Her tight-lipped frown slackened. "None of them are ugly," she said with a sigh. "But jury's out on the boring and rude."

I laughed and slung my arm around her shoulder, pulling her into a hug. "You got this. And if they give you any guff, tell them they'll have to deal with the *Red Devil*."

It was what we called my alter ego, when I let myself be at my most spitfire-y and bold (usually after a couple cocktails, let's be honest.) The Red Devil first made her appearance, though, at a sleepover in the seventh grade—no alcohol needed— when Amber Garrison mocked Kelsey in front of the entire slumber party for bleeding through her pajamas when she got her first period. I slapped her across the face and called her a mean cow. It wasn't my finest moment—and I certainly don't condone violence—but I was thirteen and defending my best friend. The Red Devil these days was a lot more fun and far less violent.

Kelsey giggled; her lips curled into a smirk. "I love it when the Red Devil comes out to play."

THE PARTY WAS BEING HELD IN THE BACK ROOM OF one of the trendy cocktail bars on Main Street called Prism. It was dark and moody, with an array of vintage-looking gold mirrors hung on the walls. Kelsey waltzed in, her head held high and confident. Nobody would be able to tell just how nervous she was inside. Classic Kelsey. But I knew it was my duty as her best friend tonight to make sure she stayed steady and kept that façade intact.

I often fell into the role of supporting character in situations. Kelsey was an effortless main character with her bubbly personality and gorgeous looks. I was the short, ginger friend with a guard up. And I loved being her best friend, so it was easy for me to assume those responsibilities. I wasn't jealous, but sometimes I did wonder when I'd be the one shining—when I'd feel like the main character. I mean, it was my life too, right?

"That's them, the rest of the events team," she said, gesturing to a cluster of people chatting, heads bowed together, looking conspiratorial.

"Go get 'em, tiger," I said with a smile.

Kelsey nodded solemnly and strode over, back straight and shoulders squared confidently. They glanced up at her and smiled politely. I'd be sure to keep my eye on them for the rest of the night.

As she did her best to charm her new colleagues, I swung by the bar and ordered a dirty martini. "Extra dirty please," I added with a smile. The woman tending bar nodded and quickly made my drink.

I positioned myself in the corner, a prime observation spot, and brought the martini glass to my lips to take a dainty sip.

"Hello there, *little lady*," a familiar, goofy twang sounded, practically right next to my ear.

I sloshed my glass, surprised, and spun around to see Derek right behind me.

"Oh shit, sorry," he said apologetically as he dug into his coat pocket and pulled out a wad of tissues and began dabbing at my now wet hand.

"Are those *used*?"

"What? No! I'm not a monster," he said, eyes wide.

"Why are they crumpled?"

"I dunno," he shrugged. "I just grab them out of the box and stuff them into my pockets."

"Of course, you do," I said, smirking. Derek seemed a little out of his element in this trendy cocktail bar. I wondered if the resort had required even the ski instructors to attend the party.

"I can get you another drink," he offered.

"There's nothing wrong with this one. It was just a little spill," I said. "But thanks."

He stood next to me in silence as we both scanned the room, watching people in chic winter-wear mix and mingle enthusiastically. My eyes landed on a swirl of people, laughing riotously. In the middle stood Cash Taylor, charming the absolute pants off of everyone in his orbit. He truly was stunning to behold—dark skin, winning smile, an expensive looking sweater hugging his chiseled shoulders and chest. No wonder people were fawning over him.

"Wow," I mused.

"That guy's really got . . . charisma," said Derek in agreement.

"Oozing it, really," I said with a laugh.

"That's a visceral way to put it." Derek smiled at me—yet another boyish grin. And, unfortunately, it made *me* smile. He really was cute, in that nonthreatening, surfer sort of way—not in the overwhelmingly handsome way like Cash Taylor. Just *very* cute. I could see why women like Nina were such big fans of him. *What woman wouldn't want a fun roll in the hay with a cute, easygoing, athletic ski instructor?* I thought, with just a hint of bitterness.

"Have you met Cash yet?" I asked.

"Briefly," Derek said with a nod. "He was very nice. Super stoked about the festival."

"Mmm," I murmured before taking a sip of my martini. It was salty and boozy, just the way I liked it.

"I'm gonna grab a beer," Derek said, heading for the bar.

Cash was talking with Kelsey and a couple other people. She caught my eye and gave me a small wave, beckoning me over. I didn't want to make small talk with her coworkers or an A-list celebrity, but for Kelsey, I would. I steeled myself and sauntered over. "This is Annie, everyone," Kelsey said with a bright smile.

"Annie, lovely to meet you," said Cash, sticking his hand out. I shook it and caught a wave of his cologne. Kelsey had been right; he *did* smell good. Notes of cedar and grapefruit, maybe a touch of sandalwood and musk, hung like an intoxicating cloud around him.

"I'm Cash." He smiled—a megawatt smile, with teeth so white they were almost blue.

"Hi Cash, nice to meet you." I smiled and then scanned the faces of Kelsey's colleagues. "I didn't catch any of your names," I prompted.

"I'm Pat," said a man with perfectly styled curly brown hair.

"I'm Yolanda," said the woman next to him. Slightly older, her hair pulled back into a chignon.

"Ellie," said the final woman. She was clearly the youngest, with a sweet round face. Her smile was looser and more genuine than the other two, whose polite smiles were tight lipped and forced.

"Nice to meet all of you . . . hope I wasn't interrupting, I'd just wanted to meet Kelsey's coworkers," I said, forcing some levity into my voice. Ellie smiled and nodded warmly at me while

Pat and Yolanda turned their attention back to Cash.

"And what were you thinking about the second night's afterparty? Is an ice luge too gauche? Too on the nose?" asked Pat. I fought back rolling my eyes.

"Ah, let's talk business tomorrow. This is supposed to be a party, isn't it?" Cash chuckled and winked at me. Against my best efforts, my stomach did the tiniest flip. Dammit, I did not want to be charmed like the rest of these people. Who cares if he was a movie star?

"Shots anyone?" asked Kelsey. Atta girl. Now this was turning into my kind of a party. Yolanda's face darkened with judgment as Pat shifted his weight awkwardly.

"Yes! That's the spirit!" said Cash. Yolanda's face quickly brightened as she smiled up at him, while Pat began to nod exuberantly.

"Yes, let's get some shots!" Pat echoed. I stifled my laughter and fought the continued urge to roll my eyes. I couldn't believe Kelsey had to work with these people.

"I'll get a tray," Kelsey said as she began heading to the bar.

"I'll help," I offered, following her, eager to not be left behind. As soon as the others were out of earshot, I let out a snicker. Leaning into Kelsey, I whispered, "Pat and Yolanda seem awful. I am so sorry."

Kelsey chuckled. "Yeah, what a couple of kiss-asses. And they're so cold to me."

"Haters," I said dismissively. "Ellie seems like she could be nice?"

"Yeah, she's sweet. A little quiet, but she's at least kind to me."

"She's probably just used to being bulldozed by those two."

"Oh, I'm *sure* of it." Kelsey leaned against the bar, waiting for the bartender. Something caught her eye, and she began waving. I glanced over my shoulder and saw Derek talking to a couple other floppy-haired guys. No doubt, they were fellow ski instructors.

"Derek, come take shots with us!" Kelsey called out. I couldn't help but be a little excited that she was pulling him into our orbit. Despite myself, I liked his company.

He walked over to us, grinning. "Shots?" He laughed and shook his head. "Never a good idea . . ."

"C'mon, don't be a party pooper," she teased. "I've got to make sure Cash has a good time. And Pat and Yolanda keep boring him with business talk . . . Please?"

Derek sighed. "Okay, fine," he said, relenting. Kelsey cheered, and he looked at me and shrugged playfully like *what-can-you-do?*

"She's impossible to say no to," I said, nodding in agreement.

Kelsey led us back to the group, tray held up high like a trophy. Yolanda eyed the liquor warily, her lips pursed tightly. But Cash beamed as he took a tiny glass from the tray. "Now *this* is what I'm talking about," he said, lifting his shot up to cheers.

Everyone followed suit and then tossed it back like champs. A wave of grimaces ran through the circle as the tequila burned its way down our throats. Next to me, Derek exhaled loudly through puckered lips. I giggled as I watched his face contort.

"I see why you stick to beer," I said, bemused. He sucked on his lime wedge intensely, shaking his head.

Cash rolled his empty shot glass between his fingers, watching us. "Annie, what do you do?"

"Oh, I don't work at Moose Creek—"

"Annie is an amazing graphic designer from New York," chimed in Kelsey. She was grinning like a proud mother as she pulled her phone out and brought up my website. "See?" She held up her screen, displaying my portfolio for all to see. I could feel my face turning red as my skin began to prickle with heat. This was so unnecessary, and now everybody was looking my way. Cash wouldn't care about my work—he was a freaking movie star.

Cash hovered over her phone, studying my designs. "Very cool . . . You know, we could use someone for the film festival logo . . . I don't know that I'm sold on what we have."

"Really?" I couldn't tell if he was just trying to make me feel good or if it was a real business proposition.

Cash nodded, smiling at me. His focus felt like a hot spotlight cast onto my face. His attention burned so bright; I could feel my cheeks begin to flush an even deeper shade of crimson. Had I really blushed this much back in New York, or did Moose Creek just bring that out in me?

"Would you be interested in talking about it over coffee?" he asked.

"Um . . ." I stammered. Derek was watching me, his head cocked to the side and his eyes narrowed. Kelsey nudged me gently with her elbow. "Yes, sure, that'd be great." I smiled, thinking of what a big opportunity this could be. *Maybe this was my main character moment!*

"Perfect, I'll get your info from Kelsey tomorrow."

"Great." I glanced at Derek; his face had gone slack. He caught me looking and tried to smile, but I could swear I saw some semblance of disdain in his eyes.

I grabbed the tray, now covered in empty shot glasses and shredded lime wedges, from Kelsey. "Here, I'll return this to the bar."

Derek followed me as I snaked through the partygoers. "He was totally hitting on you."

"No, he wasn't."

"Trust me, I know when a man is making moves."

"You don't think he could actually be interested in my skills as a designer?" It came out more defensively than I meant it to. "Also, this is none of your business!"

"What?" He shook his head vigorously, his blonde hair flopping. "No, of course, he could . . . but he could also think you're hot."

I silently handed the tray back to the bartender with a smile and turned to face Derek. I crossed my arms, daring him to say something else.

He sighed. "Your work is really good from what I saw. *Of course*, he would want to hire you."

"Mhmm," I said sarcastically. His eyes lingered on my lips, which were pursed in my best smirk. I folded my arms across my chest. "Why do you care anyway?"

Derek glanced down. "I just . . . don't want you being taken advantage of, that's all."

"That's very noble of you, but if offering me a potential job opportunity is taking advantage of me . . . I think I'm okay with it."

"I don't mean that part . . . but what if the coffee is more—never mind . . ."

I cocked my head to the side, studying his awkward stance. He looked so much stiffer than his usual aura of ease as he locked eyes with me.

"I know you can handle yourself, Annie. I just care about you, is all," he said with a forced shrug. As much as I wanted to resist it, my insides did a little twirl as he gave me a half smile. *Derek cared about me.*

Chapter 7

I SAT ON THE BENCH, BUNDLED UP IN ONE OF Kelsey's snowsuits looking like an expensive marshmallow, and waited for Derek. Looking out the windows, I could see a line of eager skiers waiting for a chairlift. A few nervous butterflies fluttered in my belly as I watched the lift glide up the mountain. *Why did I agree to this—again!?*

"Hey!" Derek's voice rang out brightly as he entered the room. He was decked out in lime green bibs, his shaggy blonde hair peeking out from his beanie. "I was worried you might bail," he teased.

"Trust me, I wish I had . . ."

"Ah, c'mon, it'll be fun." He smiled and grabbed my skis. "I'll carry these out for you."

"I can do it," I said, reaching out to grab them, but he swiped my hands away.

"Nah, it's all good. I got it." He smiled goofily and motioned for me to follow him outside. He helped me into my skis and clipped into his. "This is going to be the best, most fun ski lesson of your life!" He let out a loud whoop. "That's what I'm talking about!" His hands were waving wildly in the air as people began to eye him curiously.

I couldn't help but laugh at his forced enthusiasm, like he was trying to hype up a crowd like a motivational speaker.

Derek stopped the antics and smiled sincerely at me. "There we go. That's the sound I like."

"What sound?"

"Your laughter." My stomach flipped as he grinned at me. It was freezing out, but I was at risk of melting. *Damn you, Derek.*

He guided me to the bunny hill chairlift and held onto my elbow firmly as we boarded the lift. I clenched my jaw tight and stared straight ahead, trying not to look down.

"You got this," Derek said quietly.

I was glad he wasn't making a big deal out of my fear. I was already in a precarious mental state, just being back on the mountain again.

We approached the top, and I let out a sharp exhale in preparation for the dismount. Inside, my nerves were ricocheting through my body.

Derek silently put up the bar and gripped my elbow again, expertly steering me off the chair and out of harm's way. "You okay?"

I let out a sigh of relief and nodded tentatively.

"You remember how to stop, right?"

"Pizzas." I pushed the tips of my skis together.

"Yep. And don't forget to bend your knees. Keep that center of gravity stable."

"Okay." I gritted my teeth; I was ready to get this run over with. If I waited any longer, the fear would consume me.

"You got this! Just follow me." Derek smiled reassuringly and began to lead us down the bunny hill in large sweeping arcs.

This time no children cut in front of me. There were no disastrous collisions or mishaps. Nobody even skied close to me. I kept my eyes trained ahead, determined to get down the slope in one piece, with my dignity intact. And I did just that. In a matter of what felt like seconds to my surprise, we landed at the bottom safely. I let out a long sigh, feeling as if I'd held my breath the whole way down.

"Great job!" Derek cheered, grinning. He'd pushed his goggles up onto his forehead so I could see his blue eyes dancing like bright blue cornflowers in the midday sun. "How do you feel?"

"Better, I *think* . . . it wasn't *that* bad."

He laughed. "Okay, I guess I'll take that as a good thing. Let's go again."

I followed him back to the chairlift and up we went. I stayed focused on my breath the entire way back up. After a couple more runs, I began to feel just a *bit* more comfortable. My stomach was no longer churning inside me, and my heart was no longer in my throat, waiting for the moment I'd take a tumble. I was able to look out and enjoy the view of the mountains, which was indeed breathtaking, and sure, the mountain air was invigorating. And maybe it began to be a *little* enjoyable.

After a half hour of bunny hill skiing, I needed to rest my legs. My body was already aching. We sat outside the lodge while I rehydrated. I was in desperate need of water and gulped it down. I was about to ask Derek if we could get some hot chocolate when the ski school receptionist suddenly appeared, her face slightly frantic.

"What's wrong, Shelby?" Derek asked, rising to his feet.

"Hey, Derek, I'm so sorry but this woman is insisting on taking a lesson with you this afternoon. She even tried to pass me a hundred-dollar bill to make it happen when I told her you were busy . . ."

"Um, yeah . . . I'm with Annie now. I blocked off the rest of my day."

"I tried to tell her that, but she's being *very* persistent and offering to pay you double."

"Can't she go with Trevor?"

"She said it *has* to be you. Her friend recommended you apparently."

Derek sighed and slid his goggles up his head. He looked at me, unsure what to do. "Um . . . I don't know."

"You should take it. Double the pay?! She'll probably tip you well, too," I said. I knew what it was like to be a gig worker. You couldn't say no to double your rate.

"But you were really improving, Annie. And I was having fun." Despite myself, I felt my stomach flip at that. It was so sincere and sweet.

I laughed. "I *truly* hate to admit it, but . . . I was having fun, too."

He chuckled. "Shelby, do you think she'd be fine sharing the lesson?"

"Derek—"

"What? If she's so insistent on taking a lesson with me and unable to wait for a slot that's actually available, she can share the time with you."

"Seriously, it's really fine." Sharing a lesson

sounded awkward AF. I didn't want to freak out on the chairlift in front of a stranger.

"No," he said, sitting back down next to me. "I'm worried if I let you go now, you'll lose momentum, and I won't be able to get you back on the mountain. Shelby, see if she's okay with that?"

"I guess she has to be," she said, hurrying back inside to relay the message.

"Hopefully she says no, and we can have more time together, just us," he said, resting his hand on my thigh. I glanced down, surprised at how natural it felt. He quickly removed it and shifted in his seat.

"Don't you want the extra money, though?"

He shrugged. "Money is nice. But . . . I'm enjoying teaching you right now."

I nodded, a slight smile creeping across my face despite my effort to remain cool. "Well, you're a good teacher."

"Thanks," he said. He glanced past my shoulder and his jaw clenched. "There goes that wish . . ." I swiveled my head around and saw Shelby leading a woman towards us.

"Derek, this is Irina. She says she's just looking for a refresher . . . have a good lesson." Shelby smiled awkwardly and scurried away.

"Hello," Irina said. She was tall, with long dark hair flowing from her beanie, which was emblazoned with a Chanel logo. I wasn't great at telling people's ages, but I'd guess she was in her forties. With the amount of Botox and fillers she seemed to have injected in her face, it was hard to tell.

"Hi Irina, I'm Derek, and this is Annie."

Irina smiled at him before glancing at me. She gave me a curt, dismissive nod. *Oh boy, this was going to be interesting.*

"Well, I'm sure we can get you back on the slopes and feeling comfortable again. Annie here is a total beginner, so this will be a fun, low-pressure lesson all around."

Her eyes narrowed behind her goggles as she looked at me, dripping with disdain. It was almost comical. "I'm sure you can . . ." she said, biting her lip seductively as she eyed Derek up and down. *Wow, Irina.* Now, it was crystal clear just why she had been so insistent on having her lesson with Derek stat. She was on the hunt. What kind of reputation did Derek have in this town?

"Alrighty, then, let's get up the mountain," Derek said, a forced brightness in his voice. "We'll start with an easy green run, Lazy Susan."

"Not the bunny hill?" I piped up, my heartrate beginning to climb again.

"You're ready for this, Annie. It's an easy run, and I'll be with you the entire time." He nodded resolutely. Despite my trepidation, Derek hadn't failed me yet today, so I was just going to have to trust him.

Irina clipped into her skis with ease, and we followed Derek to another chairlift—one of the bigger ones that gave me a sinking feeling in my stomach. I took a deep breath, trying to remain calm. I *really* didn't want to freak out.

The chair scooped the three of us up—Derek sitting between us—and I worked hard to focus on my breathing. Irina, though, seemed completely relaxed. I envied her in that moment.

"It's gorgeous up here," she said with a contented sigh. I glanced over and saw she had rested a mittened hand on Derek's upper thigh. I'm sure I'd gone bug-eyed, but thankfully my goggles were tinted.

"Are you on vacation with your family, Irina?" Derek asked, his pitch climbing, as he swiped her hand away, as casually as possible. I could see he was blushing. His shoulders were square and tense, like he was bracing himself for something. I wondered, though, that if I wasn't here if he'd be more comfortable with Irina's advances. Would he have flirted back if he didn't have me as an audience?

"My family? No . . . I came out here with a

couple girlfriends. My husband works too much to go on vacation."

"Ah, that's a bummer. I bet you all would have so much fun skiing together." *Nice try, Derek.* I bit my lip to keep from laughing awkwardly.

Irina sighed heavily. "Yes, I can get very lonely . . ."

Derek didn't bother replying to that. He let out a sharp exhale and kept his eyes trained ahead. The rest of the ride was spent in silence. All the snow seemed to absorb any semblance of sound. When we got off at the top of the mountain, Irina already looked like she was in a snit. She stared daggers at me from behind her goggles.

"Okay, we can go down as slowly and as carefully as you both want to. I want you to just become reacquainted with your ski legs, Irina" Derek said.

"Yeah, yeah, I *know,*" she huffed.

"Annie, you'll follow me down the same way we did on the bunny hill. Irina, do you want to follow along as well?"

"No." Irina took off without a word. *She* didn't need a refresher or lessons at all. She began to fly down the mountain, swishing her hips back and forth in a controlled manner. No wild flailing like me. It was clear as day that she was an experienced skier.

"Wow," I said, both impressed and annoyed. Why did she have to be such a good skier?

"Sorry," Derek said with a tight-lipped smile. "That was . . . awkward, huh?"

"Yeah . . ." I bit my lip, unsure of what else to say.

"It was totally inappropriate. I should have shut it down better."

"You shouldn't have to be responsible for her behavior, though . . . I don't know. It was weird." My cheeks burned as he searched my face. I glanced down at my skis, relieved she'd left us behind. I didn't need to be followed down the mountain by a chorus of exasperated sighs. I had enough on my plate just trying to get down the mountain in one piece.

"I *am* sorry about it . . . You ready for this?" He nodded towards the trail.

I nodded. "As ready as I'll ever be . . ." Turns out, Irina hitting on Derek had been a great distraction; my nerves had somewhat dissipated.

"You got this," he said with an encouraging nod.

I followed Derek down the slope at a steady pace, carving back and forth across the trail. He narrowed our arc the farther we got, which made us gather speed. I could feel the wind begin to ripple my hair as Derek looked back at me, grinning. "You're doing amazing, Annie!"

I couldn't help but smile proudly; I was actually skiing a real run, not just the bunny hill. Derek had got me to do something I never would have thought I'd do.

Irina was waiting for us at the bottom of the mountain, looking bored. Derek sprayed a fine powder as he stopped next to her, his skis perfectly parallel. I came to a grinding halt behind him with my pizza-formation. Even behind her goggles, I could see Irina rolling her eyes at me.

"Irina, that was great. I don't think you need a refresher at all. Is there something else you want to work on?" Derek asked in his best professional voice.

"Yes . . ." she said coyly. "But it isn't skiing." Her face was windswept and rosy as she pouted her plump lips at him. *Bold move, Irina.*

"Um. Okay, well I'm a *ski* instructor, so I'm really only qualified to help you with that. I can't, like, do your taxes," he joked. He glanced at me, blushing again, his laidback air beginning to disintegrate.

Irina didn't laugh. Instead, she continued to puff out her bottom lip as she leaned towards him. "I heard you were good at other things . . ." *Wow.*

My mouth dropped open. I cannot believe she was so brazenly hitting on him like this—in front of me!? A knowing smile creeped across her face as she eyed him hungrily. Now, it was obvious to me that Derek must have a reputation for being the fun-time ski instructor, the guy always down for a good time *apres-ski*.

Kelsey had told me about these guys. Women flocked to them on vacation, looking for some action on and off the slopes. I imagined Derek grabbing cocktails in town with Irina, her long fingernails tracing his thighs, and my cheeks burned. Why was I *so* bothered by this? Watching him, I felt silly for the little crush I'd obviously developed. I reminded myself, Derek was not my type, and I *wasn't* his.

Derek shifted his weight in his skies and glanced at me, embarrassed. "Ah, well, my after-hours activities are, um, private, Irina." He gave her a tight-lipped smile, trying to stay polite and professional.

Her eyes narrowed beneath her goggles. "My friend Miriam said—"

Derek cut her off before she could say more. "Irina, I'm sorry but I can only talk to you about skiing right now. Let's keep this appropriate and professional." His voice was clipped now. A sternness I hadn't imagined he could possess took over . . . and it was kind of hot.

"Fine," she said disdainfully.

The three of us stood there in an awkward triangle. I fought the urge to laugh. "Should we do another run?" I suggested, my voice sounding two octaves higher than usual.

"Absolutely not," Irina said as she peeled off her gloves and reached into the pocket of her ski-jacket. She pulled out a fifty-dollar bill with a scrap of paper wrapped around it and handed it to Derek. "In case you change your mind . . ." She smirked confidently and glided away before he could say no.

"Wow." My mouth was yet again agape. I'd never been hit on so boldly in all my days of singledom.

"Oh god. It's her phone number," he said, reading the slip of paper.

"Of course, it is . . . are you gonna call her?" I snickered. Derek rolled his eyes, which made me relieved. He may be a playboy, but at least he didn't entertain women like Irina.

"Let's do one more run—end the day on a high note," Derek said, changing the subject.

We rode the chairlift up in silence. I imagined what Derek must be like afterhours, barhopping with the other ski instructors, running into their clients from earlier. Women in their apres-ski finest fawning over these fit and fun ski-bums, often a decade or more their junior. I'm sure it was an ego-boost. I wondered how many he'd slept with over the years. It made me blush just thinking about it.

This time down the slope, our arcs were tighter, the pace steady and quick. I kept my eyes glued on him as the wind rushed past me, biting my cheeks. It was less scary this time, as I felt the knot of nerves and urge to control loosen in my belly.

At the bottom of the run, Derek beamed proudly. "You did amazing, Annie!"

"Thanks. Like I said, you're a really good teacher." My stomach flipped a little as I watched his lips curl. *Damn that boyish grin.*

"Wanna grab a beer?" he asked. "Or would you prefer a dirty martini?"

"Huh? Don't you have more lessons?"

"No, I made sure you were my last one of the day."

My stomach flipped. Had he really scheduled his day around *my* lesson? *Play it cool, Annie.* "And I was such a difficult student you need to drink now?" I teased. He just looked at me, waiting for a response. "Um, yeah, okay. We can get a beer."

He nodded and smiled, and I swear I could see his shoulders drop as if he'd been tensing them up.

Was he nervous? Or just releasing the tension from the awkward Irina situation? I wished I could get a better read on him. The butterflies in my stomach were thundering, and I needed to know if this meant anything more than a friendly drink off the slopes.

Chapter 8

I<small>NSIDE, THE LODGE SMELLED OF FIREWOOD AND PINE.</small>
My legs were already aching from the slopes as we
sat at the bar, our knees feeling dangerously close.
Thank god for the thick layers of fabric in our ski
clothes. After my awkward afternoon with Irina, I
needed a drink. I scanned the taps, surprised by
how much I was craving a beer. Who was I now?
First skiing, and now beer?

Beside me, Derek smelled faintly of sweat and
sunscreen, and after having seen him in his element
on the slopes, it was a bit too much to bear. I felt my
body betray me with the urge to brush my thigh
even closer to his.

Derek joked familiarly with the bartender while
I covertly studied his face. His eyes were a pale blue;
they crinkled adorably when he laughed. His lightly

freckled face was open and kind, and in the right lighting, I could see fine lines etched into his forehead that betrayed his otherwise youthful appearance. His nose had a slight bend in the bridge, which I liked because otherwise he'd be too traditionally handsome, too much like the popular lacrosse and soccer players in college. The kind of guys who were happy to sleep with you and spend the night in your bed but ignored you on the quad or in class.

"So, you had a good lesson?" the bartender asked me, pulling me out of my reverie.

"Oh, yeah, Derek was great and very patient with me."

"Ah, c'mon, you conquered your fear and did it. You should be proud." That could have sounded condescending, but it didn't when coming from Derek's lips. He was surprisingly genuine and sweet.

"Good for you," said the bartender. "You gonna go again sometime?" Derek watched me carefully, his eyes hopeful.

I sighed. "Yeah . . . I actually think I would." I was surprising even myself, but I was being honest. Derek made everything . . . easier. More fun. And I hated how much I found myself liking him, feeling drawn to him. I knew this was dangerous territory. I did not want to get my heart broken—*again*. Especially by a ski bum I barely knew.

"Yes!" Derek cried out. "I did it!" He took a celebratory sip of his beer as his other hand dropped to my thigh and gave it a squeeze. Even through the puffy fabric, it sent a jolt up my leg. He quickly looked down, unsure, and removed it. I wished he hadn't.

"Not surprised. Derek's one of our best," the bartender said before helping another group of patrons.

"I paid Frank to say that," Derek joked.

"Hope you didn't give away that fifty."

"About that . . ." His jaw clenched as he studied his beer. "That was awkward and inappropriate. I'm sorry you had to see that." He looked at me sheepishly, as if he'd been the one behaving badly.

"No need to apologize. I know women can be . . . interested in that."

"God, sorry. I'm just embarrassed."

"Does that kind of stuff happen a lot?"

"A bit." He grimaced and took a swig of his beer. "I may have a bit of a reputation . . ."

"Ah, I see." I took a sip of my beer. I wasn't surprised, but I felt a sinking feeling in the pit of my stomach. If he had that kind of reputation, could I trust him and his effortless flirting? Or was it just a bit of fun for him?

"Please don't judge me."

"Why would I judge you?" I would totally be judging him—if I didn't find him so endearing. *And hot*, despite my better judgement. Hadn't our time with Irina on the slopes taught me anything?

"I can see it in your eyes." His pale blue eyes studied my face.

I shook my head, as if to wipe my expression clean. "Sorry . . . I'm just . . . not surprised, I guess?"

"Gee, thanks," he said teasingly. But his face looked wounded.

"I mean, you're a really fun guy and good looking and talented . . . of course, these women throw themselves at you." I tried to make it sound casual—like I flirted with guys like this all the time. I was backpedaling, sure, but none of what I said was untrue.

Derek smirked. "You think I'm good looking? *And* talented? *And* fun?"

"Okay don't turn this back on me now, Derek." I rolled my eyes and he laughed.

"*Aaaaannieeee*," he trilled playfully, leaning into me. My eyes traced the shape of his mouth while I fought the urge to kiss him.

"*Deeerrreekk . . .*" I mimicked.

Our faces now hung close together. Derek's gaze landed on my lips and his eyes began to glaze over. My heartbeat sounded loud as it began to echo in my ears. I eyed his mouth longingly and bit my lip, silently begging him to move an inch closer. *I would do anything to be pressed against those lips of his right now.*

"Can I get you another?" Frank interrupted, unaware of the bubble he was bursting.

"Um, yeah, sure," Derek stammered as he pulled away and tried to regain his casual composure.

I swallowed hard, trying to get a better read on the situation. *I just needed to know if Derek was flirting with me.*

Derek took a sip of his fresh pint and a sliver of foam clung to his upper lip. *Ugh,* I wanted to lick it off. "For the record, I think you're good looking too. And fun. And talented," he said, wiping the foam away with the back of his hand.

My stomach flipped excitedly. *Play it cool, Annie.* I took a long, slow sip as we locked eyes. "So, you're a bit of a playboy . . ." I imagined peeling his ski bibs off him and feeling his skin against mine. My heartbeat dropped between my legs at the thought.

He shrugged; a faint smirk etched onto his face. "Maybe . . ." *Of course, he was.*

I arched my eyebrows dramatically. "Maybe . . ." I echoed softly.

"Maybe I'm a *reformed* playboy."

"Can you playboys ever truly reform?"

"Guess you'll have to find out." He winked, and I felt my nipples stiffen. *Damn you, Derek.*

"When did you lose your virginity?"

He laughed a big, booming laugh. "What?! Where did that come from?"

I giggled and shrugged. I was feeling bold. "Dunno, just popped into my head."

"I was sixteen."

"And? Who was she? Were you in love?"

He laughed at my rapid-fire questioning. "Um, she was my high school girlfriend—"

"Name?"

"Rachel."

"*Rachel* . . . That's a hot girl name."

"A hot girl name?" Derek let out another full-throated laugh.

I smirked, pleased with myself. "Yes. I have never met a Rachel who *wasn't* hot. I bet she was hot. *And* popular."

"Are you impressed I dated the popular girl?" Derek laughed. "I mean *I* thought she was hot. I did make her my girlfriend."

"Just two all-American teenage hotties," I

teased. "*You* skied and hiked and did all the active, outdoorsy things, and I bet *she* played soccer or tennis or something."

"She was actually a cheerleader," he said sheepishly.

"A *cheerleader*!? Okay so she was *definitely* hot and *definitely* popular."

Derek laughed so hard. Despite everything, I could see he was blushing. "Well, what about you then? When did *you* lose your virginity? Was *he* hot?"

"Oh, he was *very* hot. Pale and lanky with chicken legs and a shaggy mop of dark hair." I couldn't help but giggle remembering how awkward I was as a teenager. "I thought he was beautiful, but my friends called him Dracula."

"Was he your boyfriend?"

"No, even though I thought I was *desperately* in love with him." I sighed dramatically for effect. "But alas, it was a drunken one-night thing at the end of senior year."

"Well, he was an idiot."

I shrugged. "We were young and dumb. And I've always had a thing for the quiet, brooding, noncommittal types."

"Gotta say, don't think I quite fit that mold," Derek said playfully.

"No, you really don't," I said, giving him my best flirty smile. I was so turned on by this point, I was desperate to kiss him, touch him, anything more than mere conversation.

At the door to Derek's townhouse, Coyote greeted us excitedly. Derek bent down and scratched him behind the ears as Coyote's tail wagged furiously. I took this opportunity to sneak a peek at his butt, which was by no means large or meaty, but bigger than I had expected. It looked firm and muscly, which didn't come as a surprise seeing as he skied for a living. I felt the urge to grab it and squeeze but managed to fight it. I hoped I wasn't coming off as a real creep. I didn't want to be like Irina.

Satisfied with the amount of attention he'd received from Derek, Coyote pushed past him and jumped up on me eagerly. I giggled and scratched his back with both of my hands as Derek looked at me apologetically.

"*Coyote*, down," he said, trying to be stern. I laughed harder as Coyote ignored him.

"It's fine. I love dogs!" I nuzzled my face into Coyote's neck as I pet him.

"Sorry about that. He loves attention."

"What a lovebug." I scratched his snout, and he closed his eyes blissfully. "That's good, isn't it?" I said to him softly. "What a good boy."

Derek was watching me, bemused. Coyote finally calmed down and returned to all fours. We both followed Derek into the kitchen where he opened his fridge and examined its contents. "So, I don't entertain a lot, but I do have some beer," he said.

"Beer is fine." I could care less about what we were drinking at this point.

He grabbed a couple bottles with labels I didn't recognize and opened them for us. "These are great local ales," he said, handing me one.

We clinked the necks of the bottles and took a sip without breaking eye contact. The beer was smooth and easy going down. "It's good," I said.

"Everything tastes better after a day on the slopes."

He led me into the living room to the worn leather couch. Our bodies angled towards each other as we sipped our beers. He scooched in a little more so that our knees touched, and a surge of excitement ran up my body. We kept smiling at each other; beer instantly forgotten. Derek's hand fell to my thigh. This time he didn't remove it. He looked at me with darkened eyes and my stomach flipped.

We leaned into each other as if magnets pulled together by an unseen force. Derek reached out a hand and brushed my hair out of my face, tucking a strand behind my ear, before rubbing my earlobe with his thumb and forefinger. I'd been waiting for this all day—since I watched him carry my skis for me. He pulled me to him, and our lips met. My skin felt like it was humming as he cupped his hand around the back of my head and kissed me hungrily. It was as good as I imagined. He teased my mouth open and slipped his tongue inside. A soft moan escaped me. He was a *really* good kisser.

Warmth spread through my chest and into my belly and down my arms and legs. I pressed my body into him as he wrapped his arms around me, swooping me up and maneuvering me onto his lap. I straddled him and ran my fingers through his shaggy blonde hair, trailing my nails along his scalp. He moaned softly, spurring me on. I traced my hands down his neck and across his wide shoulders. They were rigid with taut muscle. Touching him *finally* was even hotter than I could have imagined. No wonder women threw themselves at him.

Our tongues danced as I began to rock my hips back and forth against him. A low purr reverberated through me as I rolled my body into him. Even in ski pants, dry humping was fun.

Derek ran his hands down my back and grabbed my ass hungrily. "Goddamn," he said with a grunt.

"Mmmm . . ." I murmured.

"Your ass is phenomenal." His eyes glazed over wantonly as he gave me a spank and squeezed harder.

I giggled. "So I've been told . . ."

"I'm sure you have." He dove back in for more kisses as I gently caught his lip in my teeth and pulled. He groaned and kissed me harder. My skin began to prickle with heat. I ran my hands up and under his sweater; he quickly yelped. "Whoa, those are cold."

I yanked my hands back. "Sorry!"

"Here," he said, taking my hands in his. They looked so small in his as he brought them up to his mouth and blew hot air onto them. Then he kissed them before slipping them back under his sweater and returning them to his chest. "That's better."

I ran my hands over his pecks and abs—*damn, he was fit*—and began to kiss his neck, working my way up to his ear. I traced my tongue along the curve of his ear before nibbling on his lobe. He moaned and grabbed my ass harder, beginning to steer my rocking hips. His hands gripped my hips forcefully, and I knew I had to be dripping wet. A moan of pleasure escaped my lips as I grinded against him.

I undid the straps of his bibs and peeled up his sweater. He tugged it off over his head, tossing it aside on the couch. Leaning back, I admired his chiseled bare chest. It wasn't a gym rat, beefcake kind of body, but it was fit and strong. He was a natural athlete with the body to prove it.

"Wow," I murmured softly as I ran my hands over him, feeling every defined ripple of muscle.

He began to laugh, almost sheepishly.

"What?"

"You just seem so . . . in awe," he said with a chuckle.

"I am!" I gasped. "I haven't ever been with such a . . . capable man before."

"Capable?"

"Yes, your body looks very *capable*. Of many things . . ." We both began to laugh.

"Well so does yours. *Very* capable." He playfully squeezed my ass, and I squealed.

"Mhmm . . ." I murmured before pressing my lips to his. He trailed his fingers along the hem of my turtleneck, teasing my stomach. *Get these ski clothes off me already.* I was impatient, so I peeled it off for him. His eyes were glassy in that horny way men looked when they were about to get laid.

He traced his fingers along my shoulders and down my back. "May I?" he asked.

I nodded, and he unhooked my bra. I slipped it off my shoulders and let it fall to the floor.

"Wow," he said breathlessly, his face almost hypnotized. I smiled, bemused. "You are so beautiful, Annie." His eyes looked up and met my gaze. It felt like he was looking inside me, the way he stared so intently.

"So are you," I said softly. And he was. He *was* beautiful, and in a way I had never really appreciated in a man before. I pressed my body against his and kissed him hard.

He grabbed my breasts in his hands and began caressing them hungrily. It felt so good I couldn't help but moan, which just spurred him on more. He found my nipples and squeezed them tightly. I squirmed with pleasure and searched for the fly of his snow pants. When I found it, I began to unbutton, but he stopped me, grabbing my wrists in his hands. I sat up straight, taken aback.

"What?" I asked, confused.

"I don't want to move too fast," he said.

"Oh . . ." I tried to mask my confused and crestfallen face.

"Trust me, I *really* want to keep going."

"But?"

"But I like you, and I don't want this to just be like every other woman that rolls through town looking to have a fun hookup and then move on."

"Huh?" I was stunned. Was he really turning *me* down for sex? Wasn't it supposed to be the other way around?

"I know that might sound weird, and maybe I'm an idiot for not just jumping into bed with you right now . . . I mean, god, look at you!" He winced as if in pain. "But I'm not looking for just sex."

"Okay . . ." It was like my brain couldn't compute. I was confused and disappointed. He'd said it himself that he was a playboy and had a reputation. And I'd witnessed firsthand how women reacted to him. But he didn't want me like that, I guess, and it stung.

"I had a really good day with you," he said.

I nodded slowly, still processing, and climbed off his lap. Locating my turtleneck, I pulled it back on over my head and held my bra in my fist. My face felt hot, and I was worried I might begin to cry from embarrassment. I turned away so he wouldn't see me like that.

"Annie, I'd like to see you again."

I spun around to face him. "Really?"

"Yes, really." He began to laugh softly. "I wouldn't say that if I didn't mean it."

I narrowed my eyes, studying his face. He looked so kind; I really wanted to trust him, but he'd just rejected me.

"Don't look so skeptical! C'mere," he said, patting the sofa next to him. I sat down next to him, quiet. He wrapped an arm around me, pulling me towards him and kissing me sweetly on the lips. "Let me take you skiing again this weekend," he said with an impish grin.

I began to laugh. "This was all a part of your evil plan to get me back on the slopes!" I slapped his chest playfully.

He flashed a mischievous smile and threaded his hands around my waist, giving me another kiss. "Just say yes."

I groaned. "Ugh, fine, alright! I'll do it!"

He cheered goofily as I rolled my eyes and pouted dramatically. "You're cute when you pout," Derek said.

"I know," I said with a satisfied smirk.

Chapter 9

I slipped inside the house as Kelsey was giving Noah a bath. "Hey," she called out from upstairs. "Come up here!"

In the bathroom, she was hunched over Noah who was spastically waving a rubber duckie around. "Where've you been?"

"Next door . . ." I said coyly.

"With Derek?" Her eyebrows furrowed as she smiled knowingly. "So, the ski lesson went well I take it."

"It was better than I had expected. *Almost* fun."

"Good . . ." she said, eyeing me as Noah played in the shallow bathwater.

"Yep . . ."

"Must have been a *long* ski lesson. What time did you even start? 2pm?"

"I'm a slow learner, what can I say?"

"*Annie,*" she said with a giggle. "How did you end up back at his place?"

I sighed but couldn't help smiling as I sat down atop the closed toilet. "He asked me to grab a drink after the lesson—which, by the way, was crashed by a *very* horny woman named Irina."

"What do you mean 'crashed?'"

I launched into a full retelling of my day as Kelsey bathed Noah. She was amused, but unsurprised by the woman's behavior. "It happens more often than you'd think," she said.

But once I reached the kiss, she squealed, her eyes wide. "I knew it!"

"Knew *what?*"

"That he liked you! It was so obvious. He was so annoyed that Cash asked you to coffee. And the way he looks at you when you aren't paying attention . . . it's very cute."

"Really?" I could feel my cheeks blushing as a smile plastered its way onto my face. No sense in playing it cool for Kelsey, I guess.

"Yes, really!" She was elated—seemingly more so than I was.

"He didn't want to have sex though."

"Annie, you tried to have sex with him?!"

"Of course! He was a really good kisser, and I was turned on, so what?!"

"Hey, no judgment from me, I'm just surprised you went for it. He's not your usual type—which for the record, I think is a *good* thing."

"Ugh, stop," I sighed. "But it seems like he'll give it away to any lady that comes through Moose Creek but me," I said, shaking my head, feeling bitter. My ego was still bruised, and I wasn't sure how long I'd be salty.

"Maybe you're more than just sex to him."

"Ugh," I groaned. "Maybe . . . he does want to take me skiing again."

"Well, good! That's promising."

I nodded but wasn't sure I was convinced. Old habits die hard and after our run-ins with Nina and Irina, I was sure he was used to having fun with just about any woman that struck his fancy. Seemed like life was a sexual smorgasbord for Derek. And I just wasn't on the menu.

CASH WAS SEATED IN THE CORNER OF THE LODGE, a well-fitted sweater clinging to his perfectly chiseled chest. In all the commotion with Derek, at home and on the slopes, I'd almost forgotten I was due to hang out with a bona fide movie star. Cash stood as

I approached the table, like a true gentleman, and shook my hand firmly. I couldn't help but be struck by the stark differences between he and Derek. He was no local ski bum, that's for sure. "Thanks for meeting me," he said with a winning Hollywood smile. His teeth were dizzyingly white in the morning sun and absurdly straight. I wondered if they were veneers. Did real people even have teeth that perfect?

"Of course, thank you for inviting me," I said with a nod. "I'd love to hear more about what it is you don't like about the festival's current logo and what you're looking for instead." I sat down and ordered a latte from the server, who was *very* attentive thanks to Cash's celebrity.

"Great." He pulled out his laptop and began showing me the image files. The logo was generic and bland, too boxy and angular. "Too masculine. Too corporate," he said. I nodded along as he pointed out its flaws. "I want something that fits the vibe of Moose Creek but marries it with cinema. If we're going to be uplifting and celebrating independent filmmakers while also serving the community and attracting visitors, I want it to be accessible and welcoming, but still chic." I appreciated his insight. It was so clear he cared about this festival.

"Got it." I held out my hands towards his computer. "Do you mind?"

"Not at all," he said, pushing it towards me.

I googled Moose Creek Mountain and began scrolling the image search results. "So, Moose Creek Mountain's branding has a very vintage, quaint feel to it. Which is incredibly different from the festival's current branding—obviously. I do think there is a way to make the design capture the nostalgic vibes of the ski resort but have it still feel fresh and recognizable as a film festival. I'll need to think on it, but right off the bat, I think we use a matching, retro font but make it a bit thinner, more modern."

"I like that idea . . ."

"And for the logo, I'd nix the basic acronym logo MCFF . . . I think it's been done, and you're right, it doesn't capture the essence of what you want. I can draw up some ideas and get them to you in the next few days?"

He was smiling and looking at me sideways.

"What?"

"I'm just impressed. You're straight to business and know exactly what to do."

"What did you expect? You didn't think I'd be professional?" I immediately regretted it the moment I said it.

"No, no, no. I'm sorry, I didn't mean it like that." Cash shook his head seriously. "I'm just new to this and am used to people blowing smoke up my ass, or not taking my ideas and feedback seriously."

"Oh." I let out a little sigh. "Sorry, I got defensive . . . I totally understand."

"People just look at me as some actor, not as a businessman or someone who could possibly run a film festival." His eyes were round and sincere as he looked at me. I felt my shoulders relax; I didn't need to prove myself to him. Maybe Cash and I had more in common than I realized.

"That must be frustrating," I said, looping my fingers around my warm mug.

"It can be, yes." He let out a soft chuckle and took a sip of his coffee. "Seems like you might be able to relate."

"Not on such a public scale," I joked. "But yeah, I find myself feeling like I have to fight to be taken seriously sometimes with work. Especially with older male clients. They often talk to me like I'm a little girl who couldn't possibly understand what they *really* mean."

He nodded, empathetic. "Well, from what I saw of your portfolio the other night, you're clearly talented and good at what you do. I'm excited to see what you come up with and would love to hire you if it works out."

"That would be great." I took a sip of my latte and explained to him my rates and process. Usually, I'd take a deposit up front, but since this was related to Kelsey's job—and Cash was a real-life movie star —I didn't mention it. He jotted down a few notes in a small leather-bound notebook before tucking it away in his bag.

"Well, I've got to jet, but thanks for meeting with me, Annie." He rose to his feet and gave my hand one last firm shake. "I've got a talk show appearance back in LA and need to catch a flight. Talk soon?"

"Sounds good," I said with a nod.

"Fantastic." He flashed another megawatt smile and strode away. I'm sure he had a town car waiting for him outside, ready to whisk him off to the nearest airport.

THAT AFTERNOON, I NESTLED INTO THE COGNAC leather armchair and perched my tablet on my knees. I began to doodle, brainstorming what elements I may want to include in the new design for the Moose Creek Film Festival. Did I want to include the silhouette of the mountain? Its towering evergreens shimmering with snow? The outline of its large timber lodge?

With each line I drew, I had a harder and harder time focusing. My brain kept flashing to the other day with Derek. His lips on mine. The way his tongue slipped inside my mouth. His hands running through my hair and sliding down my body. Feeling him hard and lustful even beneath the layers of clothing. I shook my head as if to scatter these dirty thoughts away, but it didn't work. Even though I'd just had coffee with a movie star, I couldn't get Derek out of my mind. My skin felt tingly, desperate to be touched by him again.

I glanced at the fireplace. It was cold and unlit, but a few logs remained neatly stacked next to it. Without second guessing myself, I got up and threw my coat and boots on and skipped over to Derek's. A few quick knocks sent Coyote howling excitedly before Derek swung the door open. His face cracked wide into a toothy grin. "Well, this is a pleasant surprise."

"Hi. Um, could you build me another fire?"

"Guess you didn't learn from my first demo," he teased.

"I'm a slow learner," I said with a shrug.

"I think you just want an excuse to see me . . ." I bit my lip fighting the urge to kiss the self-satisfied smirk off his face. He chuckled and grabbed his coat. "Of course, I'll build you a fire. Anything you want. Anything you need." My stomach flipped and my cheeks flushed. I couldn't help but smile as we walked back to Kelsey's townhouse.

"I do have one condition, though," Derek said as he opened the front door for me, ever the gentleman.

"Oh?"

"I get to stick around and enjoy the fire with you." He smirked and ran his hands through his shaggy blonde hair. I wanted to thread my own hands through his thick hair and pull him close to me.

"Hm, only seems fair, I guess," I said coyly.

"I think so." He flashed me that signature boyish grin that was now seared into my memory. *Damn you, Derek.* I was in trouble. My baser nature had taken over and all I wanted was to touch him, taste him, smell him. I wanted to feel every inch of his skin against mine, his taut muscles hard against my soft body. I took in a sharp inhale, willing myself to be cool.

"You okay?" Derek asked, bemused at my flushed cheeks.

"Uh-huh." I nodded as I watched him carefully. He bent over, stacking the wood skillfully. His sweatshirt was bunched up to his elbows, showing off his forearms. Those forearms that I desperately wanted wrapped around my waist. He could squeeze me like a boa constrictor for all I cared . . . I was practically salivating over him. He lit the kindling, and a crackling pierced the air. I loved the sound of fire.

Derek swiveled around and reached his hand out, tucking a loose strand of hair behind my ear affectionately. "Better?" he asked.

I nodded, unable to break eye contact with his pale blue gaze. Tilting my chin up towards him, I silently begged him to kiss me. Cupping my face in his hands that smelled of firewood, he leaned in and did just that. It was a gentle kiss at first. Our lips softly feeling each other out. I took a step closer to him, and he skated his hands down to my hips, gripping them as he pressed his body into mine. Our lips parted and our tongues began to dance with a building intensity.

I ran my hands across his back and down to his ass, grabbing a handful hungrily. It sent a thrill down my spine. I could feel that I was already wet, especially after fantasizing about him earlier. I steered him towards the couch, desperate to straddle him and push my body against his, letting the friction tickle me in all the right places.

He grunted softly in between kisses and spun

me around, taking charge. He pushed me onto the sofa, grabbing my thighs with ease and parting them. His eyes darkened with desire as he traced his fingertips along my legs and up the seam of my pants. I rolled my hips forward as a soft, needy moan escaped my lips. He lightly lingered right on the space above my clit, hovering as if to taunt me. I groaned. He bit his lip and continued to trail them up my stomach and finally to my breasts. I was panting now, my body hot, craving him. He circled my nipples with his thumbs as they stiffened. My body squirmed, wanting more. He smirked cockily; he was determined to tease me.

"Kelsey's upstairs with Noah," I whispered, my voice thick.

"Don't worry, nothing's gonna happen here."

"Huh? What?"

Derek laughed softly, pleased with himself and this power he held over me. I wanted to roll my eyes, but I was too distracted by the feel of his fingers now pinching my nipples firmly through the wool of my sweater.

"No chance in hell I'm rushing this," he said softly, his voice gravelly.

"Please . . ." I begged.

He leaned down and kissed me gently on the lips, then on the forehead as he released my nipples.

He sat down on the couch, watching me trying to pull myself back together. What was he doing to me? This felt like torture. I was so turned on, it felt like an ache—a very painful ache. I groaned frustratedly as I sat up and caught my breath. He was smiling, bemused.

"Don't look so self-satisfied," I said bitterly.

He laughed. "I'm not doing this to torture you, I promise."

"Yeah, right," I rasped "It's mean to tease me like this. You'll give it away to every other woman in Moose Creek but me?!" Immediately I regretted saying it. His face stiffened, lips tight and jaw clenched. "I'm sorry, Derek, I didn't mean it like that."

He sighed. His hands were balled into his fists. He caught me looking and consciously unclenched them, smoothing them over his knees. "I don't want it to be like that with you."

"I know, I'm not the kind of girl you go for. Plus, wouldn't want to make it awkward with Kelsey being your new neighbor . . ."

"What?" He shook his head, brow furrowed. "No, it's not that."

"I don't get it then, I guess." I sighed, exasperated and still very sexually frustrated. Was I not attractive enough for him? Sexy enough? It seemed like he was enjoying himself . . . the kisses were certainly good. How could I be reading this situation wrong?

Derek opened his mouth, about to speak, when Kelsey bounded down the stairs. "Oh, hi," she said, taking note of his sudden appearance in her living room. She glanced at the fireplace and her face spread into a delighted smile. "A fire! Oh my god, I love it!" She set the baby monitor down on the coffee table and plopped herself into the leather armchair.

"I enlisted Derek's expertise again," I said, smoothing my hair back down.

"It's wonderful. Thanks, neighbor!"

"You're welcome, neighbor." They both chuckled.

I felt a pang of jealousy that was *not* warranted. It wasn't like he was suddenly going to hit on Kelsey just because he rejected me. *Again.*

"Oh, are these some of your ideas for the new logo?" asked Kelsey, picking up my tablet from the coffee table.

"They're just doodles . . . I was brainstorming."

"I wanna see." Derek got up and hovered over Kelsey's shoulder as he examined the screen.

"They're really just scribbles—"

"These are great, Annie. I love them," said

Derek, glancing over at me with a smile. Seemed genuine enough, but I wasn't ready to move on from what had just happened. I felt so foolish and unwanted. Did he get off on making me want him like that and then denying me? And then acting all kind and sweet after? Like he hadn't just rejected me and seriously bruised my ego. Was this some kind of power trip? Or was I a charity case?

"I knew you could do better than what they had," said Kelsey proudly.

"Well, those really are just me doodling out ideas . . . going to solidify them into a few different options to present to Cash."

"I'm sure he'll love whatever you come up with," said Kelsey.

Derek nodded in agreement. "I'll get out of your hair."

"Oh, please stay," Kelsey insisted. She glanced at me and gave me the faintest smile. *Please don't stay, please don't stay.* I just wanted to forget about what had just happened on the couch. "I was just going to order us a pizza for dinner. Want some?"

"Yeah? Alright, that sounds great, thanks." Derek looked at me and smiled, chuffed. I couldn't help but frown. He cocked his head to the side, confused. I pouted and turned away. I didn't want to eat pizza with him right now.

While Annie slipped into the kitchen to place the order, Derek paced towards me. "What's wrong?" he asked in a hushed voice.

"Nothing," I said. *Real mature, Annie.*

"You're acting weird. Did I do something?" He searched my face, his eyes wide with concern. Was he joking? Or was he really that oblivious?

"Are you serious?"

"Yes, I don't understand what happened. I thought we were having a good time."

My jaw dropped. He really was dense. "We *had* been having a good time. Until you totally played me on the couch. A girl can only handle so much rejection." My voice was a sharp whisper. My throat felt tight and dry. I turned on my heel and went into the kitchen to get water. Derek stood frozen in the living room, his face dumbfounded.

"Pizza should be here in thirty," announced Kelsey as I grabbed a glass from the cabinet.

"Great." I filled it to the brim and then gulped it down hard, before turning the faucet back on for a refill.

I followed Kelsey back into the living room where Derek was hunched over the fireplace, stoking the embers. With a few magic pokes and prods, the fire turned roaring quickly. He sat back on his haunches, admiring his work. I had to pull my eyes away from ogling his rear. I should have never kissed a guy like him. I knew better. *Guys like him would only make you feel like an idiot, Annie.*

Kelsey was watching me, brow furrowed. When I caught her eye, she mouthed *What's going on with you?* I shrugged and tried to wave away her concern. I wasn't sure she'd understand. And honestly, I didn't want her to defend Derek or try to romanticize the situation. She could always see the best in people. But then again, men were often falling over themselves to even look at her, let alone touch her or kiss her.

The three of us sat on the couch for the next thirty minutes, admiring the fire and making small talk. Well, Derek and Kelsey did most of the talking, with me only chiming in occasionally. I was doing my best not to pout, but I was in a bit of a snit. It had been such a long time since a man had gotten under my skin like this . . . usually the sexy, physical part was easy and the actual emotional and mental connection was harder to draw out of them. Had I been putting too much stock into sex? I don't think so . . . I mean, Derek had been the one to pinch my nipples and hover over my jeans so teasingly. Just thinking of that fleeting moment sent a flutter between my legs and in my stomach.

Eating pizza, watching my best friend and my

new crush gab away, I nearly burned the roof of my mouth. Derek laughed at my dramatic reflex, pulling my slice away and yelping. Against my best effort, I smiled and laughed with him. His eyes seemed to twinkle as he watched me with his lips curled up playfully. *Damnit, why did he have to be so cute?* He took a big bite of his pepperoni slice and I had to quell the urge to lean across the table and lick the lingering sauce above his top lip.

"What?" he asked, noticing my eyes affixed to his mouth.

"Oh, uh, you have some sauce," I said, running my fingertip across my upper lip. "Right there."

"Here?" He swiped the back of his hand across his mouth, smearing the sauce across his mouth and onto his cheek. "Better?"

"Now it's on your cheek," I said with a giggle. Kelsey began to laugh as Derek only made more of a mess, rubbing the sauce all over the side of his face.

"Did I get it?" There was a mischievous glint in his pale blue eyes as he cocked his head to the side, as if to challenge me.

I shook my head with a faux exasperated sigh.

"Why don't you just get it for me?"

I grabbed my napkin and leaned over, hovering close to him. My pulse quickened as I scanned the light freckles across his cheek and began cleaning up the sauce on his face. I had to lick the napkin to get it all up.

"I like this," he said, almost under his breath. He leaned in closer so that it tickled my ear. Did he get off on torturing me like this? My skin prickled. All I wanted to do was whisk him upstairs and ride him until I passed out.

I quickly sat back in my chair and took a deep breath. Kelsey was watching me, bemused. My face flushed, and I grabbed my water, downing it thirstily, hoping it would cool me down.

"Thirsty much?" Kelsey teased.

"I guess so." I got up and refilled my glass with more cool water from the tap. As I turned around, I saw Derek quickly look away. I *knew* he'd just snuck a glance at my ass.

We finished the pizza fast, practically licking the greasy box clean. And as the delicious carbs and cheese settled in my stomach, I was ready to hibernate.

"Well . . . this was delicious. Thanks for having me," Derek said, getting up and stacking the plates on top of one another.

"Of course. Anytime." Kelsey smiled as she watched him load the dishwasher.

"How much do I owe you?" he asked.

"Oh, don't worry about it."

"Well, I'll get you all next time then."

I wasn't sure I wanted there to be a next time. I don't know if I could handle it. My nervous system already felt so confused and frayed from the past few hours. How many emotions could I cycle through in the span of mere hours, all because of one man? Excited, amused, horny, rejected, embarrassed, angry, sad, hurt, rinse, repeat all over again. I was exhausted.

"You okay, Annie?"

"Huh?" I was staring at the table, lost in my own head. I looked up and saw Kelsey and Derek both looking at me, as if studying me.

"You went somewhere else for a moment there," Kelsey said with a chuckle.

"Just was asking if you were okay, that's all," said Derek with a reassuring smile.

"Yeah, just tired. Lots of pizza. Long day . . . you get it."

"Annie can sometimes get lost in that beautiful brain of hers," said Kelsey lovingly.

"I can see that . . ." Derek said, nodding. "Beautiful brain indeed."

I shrugged and glanced down at my feet.

"Well, I should get going." Derek got up and gave Kelsey a hug. He paused in front of me. I got out of my chair and wrapped my arms around him, as if being conducted by a set of marionette strings. He held me close for a second too long. His body was warm and firm as it pressed against me. I had to take a step back before I could tip my chin up to kiss him.

"Goodnight," I said softly.

"Goodnight." His eyes lingered on mine until we both realized Kelsey was standing right there, watching us with a bemused smile on her face.

"Alright then." He gave a curt nod and grabbed his coat by the door. "See ya. Thanks again for the pizza." And off he went.

Kelsey burst into amused laughter once the sound of his footsteps had faded completely. "You're screwed."

"What?!"

"Annie, I know you better than I know myself, and you're smitten with him."

"I am *not*!"

"Please! You're all moody and in your head and acting as if he couldn't *possibly* like you back. It's what you do."

"I do *not*!"

"Yes, you do! And you have been that way since middle school. Even when the guys are totally smitten with you too. Remember Jeremy?"

I sighed and nodded slowly as I plopped myself down onto the couch, feeling defeated. Jeremy was my on-and-off-again college boyfriend. I'd get so into my head and convince myself that he wasn't as into me as I was into him. I was so scared of getting hurt and rejected that I pushed him away. My brain would just spiral out of control, even though Jeremy gave it no reason to. He was perfectly lovely and affectionate and kind. But I read into every move he made, every word he said. I was exhausted with myself but felt like I couldn't stop it.

"Ugh," I groaned loudly. "Maybe you're right."

"Of course, I'm right!"

"But I don't like Derek like that."

"Bullshit."

"I'm serious . . . I'm just attracted to him. He's sexy and fun. But that's *all* it is."

"Mhmmm," she said, nodding her head sarcastically.

I rolled my eyes. "I mean it. And besides, he's not even into me like that. He just gets off on teasing me."

"What are you talking about? You kissed! It's so *obvious* he likes you. I mean, the way he looks at you, for Christ's sake. It's practically pornographic."

"That's just who he is. He's a total playboy! He's the George Clooney of Moose Creek."

Kelsey laughed and shook her head. "Even George fell in love with Amal, and they're married with kids now."

"You know what I mean."

"Yeah, so maybe you're his Amal," Kelsey said with a smirk.

I sighed. "I'm definitely not. I'm not even a steppingstone to Amal. I'm a passing fancy, an amusement for him to play with and tease. He likes to lord his sexual power over me, but he doesn't actually want to be with me or even sleep with me."

"Fine," Kelsey said with an exasperated sigh. "If that's what you want to believe, Annie. I can't force you to get out of your own way." *Ouch.* It stung hearing Kelsey say those words, even if they were the truth that I didn't want to admit.

Chapter 10

DESPITE DEREK DOMINATING SO MUCH OF MY thoughts, I'd managed to narrow my logo designs for Cash down to three. The third option was my personal favorite. I thought it was some of my best work, maybe ever. It was cute and vintage without being too kitschy, but really resonated with the feel of Moose Creek. I could see it being a hit on merchandise. People scooping up branded t-shirts and sweatshirts, beanies and baseball caps, the logo would even look great printed down the leg of a pair of sweatpants. A good logo like that on quality merchandise just meant more money for both the resort and the film festival.

I was excited to present the final designs and walked into the lodge with confidence. I hadn't felt like this in a long time . . . and I hadn't even been hired yet. It wasn't guaranteed he'd even like my logos, but I knew it would be his mistake if he didn't use me.

Kelsey had pumped me up the night before our meeting. She couldn't stop raving about them and how they'd elevate the whole event. And Kelsey doesn't bullshit me—as evidenced by the other night. It still baffled me that of all places in the world, Moose Creek was where I might be getting my biggest career break yet. Somehow, in this tiny, snowy town, life was moving fast for me. And *that* was exciting.

Grabbing one of the leather couches by the fire, I sat down and placed the printouts of my designs on the coffee table. The lodge had just opened. The morning was already bright and sunny, and the first few skiers could be seen boarding the chairlifts outside.

Frank, the bartender, stood behind the bar across the large dining room, polishing glasses. I was early for my meeting with Cash, as always. But I wasn't as anxious as I'd anticipated. I could risk the caffeine, even with my nerves, so I strode over to the bar and ordered a coffee.

"Could I see the designs?" Frank asked excitedly.

"How did you know?" I was surprised he even

remembered who I was, let alone that I was pitching a new logo for the film festival.

"Oh, nothing's kept secret here. Word travels fast." He handed me a steaming cup of coffee and a tiny pitcher of cream. I poured it in slowly, watching it swirl into the liquid until it was the perfect caramel color.

"Sure," I said with a nod.

Frank followed me back to the fireplace, my glossy designs spread out on the table. "Holy shit, these are good!" He sounded genuinely surprised. I laughed. "So much better than what they had before."

"Let's hope Cash likes them as much as you do."

"If he doesn't, he's an idiot." Frank smiled at me, before heading back to the bar. I *knew* they were good. But it never hurt to get the enthusiastic approval of another person.

I positioned myself forward, feeling confident, as I sipped my coffee and studied the designs intently. Frank was right. They were good. And Cash *would* be an idiot if he didn't hire me.

"Hello, hello!" A booming baritone voice filled the mostly empty room. It was the kind of voice you knew immediately. And not just from the movies, practically every car and insurance commercial seemed to use his rich and distinct voice. Cash was beaming and looking ever the dapper movie star in his perfectly tailored navy peacoat and jeans, with snow boots that looked as though they somehow magically hadn't even touched the snow yet. It wasn't surprising to me that he looked so perfect.

"Hi!" I stood and he strode over, shoulders square and confident as he reached out his hand to shake mine.

"Whoa!" He glanced down at the designs mid-handshake. "These are *incredible,* Annie." He dropped my hand and leaned over the coffee table, examining the three new logos.

"Oh god. Thank you . . . I'm so glad you like them." I sat back down on the couch. He continued to study them quietly, as I watched him closely. I couldn't stop tapping my foot as my anticipation grew. "Can I get you a coffee, by the way?"

"Sure. Just black."

Frank handed me Cash's order, throwing me a quick wink before I turned on my heel. I fought the urge to throw my fists into the air triumphantly. But he hadn't *yet* given me the job.

I carefully set Cash's coffee down on the edge of the table, careful to keep away from my printouts.

He sat down wordlessly and grabbed his coffee, eyes locked on my work.

After a long sip of his coffee, he finally looked up at me. "Well, obviously, you're hired."

A surge of excitement and pride flooded my body. I wanted to jump up and down, but instead, just smiled gratefully. "Amazing. Thank you so much. I'm so excited to work on this project with you." Was Moose Creek my new good luck charm? It felt like I'd been stuck in a cycle of the same gigs, the same men even, until I landed here.

"Me too." Cash's eyes crinkled warmly as he smiled back at me. "And this," he said, tapping the third design—my personal favorite— "is perfect. It *has* to be the new logo."

I grinned and took a sip of my coffee. "I *totally* agree. It's my favorite too. And I think it would look so good on any merchandise you plan on selling—sweatshirts, hats, really anything you can think of."

"It's going to be *iconic*."

"That's high praise," I said with a laugh.

"It's great work." Then, he skimmed through the contract and paperwork and image rights. His business manager would send over everything I needed to read and sign. I nodded along, making sure my enthusiasm wasn't bursting at the seams and therefore, off-putting and unprofessional. It had to be just the right amount of enthusiasm. Cash didn't need to know that this would be the biggest get of my career so far. And the most lucrative.

As our meeting wrapped up, Cash gathered the images into the folder I'd brought. "I can take these, right?" he asked.

"Of course."

"Great." He put his coat on and slid the folder underneath his arm neatly. "How about a congratulatory dinner this weekend? I have to go back to LA for a couple days but will be back on Saturday."

"Oh, um . . . you totally don't have to do that . . ." I'd never had a client take me out for dinner before. Was this normal? Or was he . . . hitting on me? Maybe it was just common practice in Hollywood? Big celebratory dinners and all that . . .

"I insist. Honestly, your work is just going to make me look better," he said with a chuckle. "We're in this together now."

"Oh. Uh. Okay, dinner would be lovely. Thank you." He was too charismatic to say no. Plus, who didn't want to go to dinner with Cash Taylor?

"My assistant will text you with the details later."

"Great."

He shook my hand firmly and headed back into the cold. I let out a deep exhale that I felt I'd been holding in for days. I wanted to ricochet off the walls from all the nervous, antsy energy I'd been bottling up. My work had paid off and now I wanted to let it free.

"It's okay if you want to scream or dance or something," called out Frank from behind the bar. "Nobody else is in here and you deserve to be excited."

I nodded and let out a loud whoop. It filled the room, almost echoing through the tall beams of the ceiling. It felt good, so I did it again. Frank laughed. "Too early for a celebratory drink?"

"Yeah, I think 9am is a *little* early for me." I smiled and plopped back down onto the couch. As I watched the fire crackle and pop, I sipped my coffee. For the first time in a long time, I felt content. I couldn't wait to tell Kelsey, of course, but I wanted to savor this moment just for myself. Afterwards, I could slip upstairs to her office and tell her the good news. Right now, this moment of celebration was just for me.

A few people trickled in and ordered coffees from Frank. I'm sure I looked silly, sitting by myself and grinning from ear to ear, just watching the fire roar. I felt my cheeks start to ache, but I couldn't stop smiling.

This job could catapult my career. It would be a huge win for my portfolio. I could raise my prices and afford to be choosier about the kinds of gigs I took. I'd been grinding in New York for years— almost a decade now—hustling and taking any project I could get my hands on.

I returned my coffee cup to Frank and headed upstairs. I wasn't exactly sure where Kelsey's office was, other than on the second floor, and began roaming the hallway, carefully scanning the plaques next to each door.

"You lost, little lady?" a familiar, horrible faux-twang echoed down the hallway. I glanced up and sure enough, it was Derek. His sun-bleached hair perfectly floppy, a cockeyed smirk plastered to his face.

"You really are *bad* at accents. Dismal, really," I said.

"What are you talkin' 'bout?" Except it sounded like wut-err-yeow-tah-kin-beowt.

"Was that even English?"

He shrugged and laughed. I joined in. *Damn your charms, Derek.*

"Were you looking for me?" he asked, running his hands through his mop of hair.

"Huh?"

"Thought maybe you were wandering these halls, trying to hunt me down." He flashed a devilish grin.

I rolled my eyes. "No, I'm looking for Kelsey."

"Ah, of course . . . she's the third door to the left." He led me down the hall and rapt his knuckles on her door three times.

"Come in!" her voice cried out, muffled.

He swung the door open. "Special delivery!"

"Annie! How did it go?" Kelsey squealed, rising from her desk.

"Amazing! I got the job. He loved my designs—and picked my favorite." I beamed proudly as Kelsey jogged around her desk and wrapped me in her arms tightly.

"I knew he would!!" I inhaled her rose perfume, the same scent she'd been wearing since we were fourteen. Somehow, it aged perfectly with Kelsey. It smelled like her at fourteen, and it still smelled like her at thirty. Anytime I caught a whiff, a pang of comfort and home hit me in the solar plexus.

Derek was standing in the doorframe still, watching us. "I take it this is about the logos for the big new film festival?"

Kelsey and I dropped our arms, both grinning

still. I swiveled to face him and nodded. "Yessssss! I got it!"

"Congratulations!" His smile was genuine and wide, not a trace of teasing in his pale blue eyes. It made my stomach somersault. "We should celebrate tonight," he said.

"Yes, yes, yes! We have to!" Kelsey nodded enthusiastically. "I can get my mom to watch Noah. We could actually *go out*!"

"Yeah?" I asked. It *did* sound like fun.

"Please, I'd love an excuse to get dressed up and not sit at home in my breastmilk-stained sweats."

"Let's do it, then," said Derek resolutely.

Kelsey clapped her hands excitedly as she sat back in her desk chair. "It's settled. Derek, meet us at our place at 7."

"Roger that. See you ladies later." He gave us a rakish wink and turned on his heel, his footsteps echoing throughout the hall.

Kelsey turned to me and smiled mischievously. "Maybe tonight's *the* night . . ." She wriggled her eyebrows as she cooed.

"Yeah, right. He's just a flirt, that's all."

Kelsey rolled her eyes. "Sure, sure . . . now go home and have a nice soak in the hot tub or something. You deserve it."

"Good idea!"

"And call your mother to tell her the good news!"

"God, has she been bugging you?"

"No, but she does text me about the baby. You know she loves it when I send her photos of Noah."

I sighed. "I know, I know . . . she's desperate for grandbabies."

"She is." Kelsey's face softened. "But she loves you for you, Annie. Don't let it get to you. It's just what moms do."

I shrugged. "I don't remember Dina pressuring you to pop 'em out."

"That's because I married Rick, notorious asshole."

"Fair enough," I said with a laugh.

The hot tub bubbled like a witch's cauldron as I jogged across the deck. A steady stream of steam unfurled from its surface, beckoning me. I slung my towel across the side and slowly slid into its hot, soothing water. A low sigh escaped my lips dramatically. God, it felt *good*. As I sank lower, my muscles began to relax, and I realized I'd been *so* tense. Sure, I was confident about my designs. But there was a lot of potential riding on this opportunity. I don't think I had wanted to admit just how anxious I had been, even to myself.

The sky overhead was grey and heavy with looming snow. Pine trees and evergreens surrounded the townhouse complex, their branches ready to catch snowflakes.

My phone sat on the edge of the tub next to my towel. I picked it up gingerly and called my mom, setting it back down on the edge, turning on speaker phone.

She picked up on the second ring. "Hi dear!"

"Hi mom, how are you?"

"Oh, I'm fine, but do you remember Teri? The woman who volunteered at the library and had an affair with the mayor?"

"No?"

"Yes, you do! She would feed all the stray cats by the train tracks."

"Oh, *of course*, Teri, yes. How could I forget?" I did not remember her in the slightest.

"Ah, well. She died."

"I'm so sorry to hear that . . . were you two close?"

"No, not at all. I think she cheated at bridge and could be a nasty drunk."

"Oh."

"But it's always sad when someone you know

dies." She said it so matter-of-factly, without an ounce of actual grief. I laughed softly under my breath. Mom could be such a gossip.

"Yeah, you sound real cut up about it."

"Oh, Annie, don't be fresh with me now . . . any-who, how are you, dear?"

"I'm good, mom. I actually called to tell you some good news—"

"You're pregnant?!" she squealed excitedly. "I knew it!"

"Mom, I don't even have a boyfriend."

"So? Women are sexually liberated these days! You don't need a boyfriend to get pregnant."

"Wow, you really are desperate."

"Please, honey, you're almost thirty-one. I can't hold my breath. I just want a little grandbaby!"

I exhaled sharply. "Nope, not the news I called to tell you, sorry to let you down." There was a sting in my voice that I hated hearing. Even though she was half joking, my mom could cut to the core.

"Oh, well, maybe someday, dear . . ."

"I was calling to tell you I got a really cool job. I'm doing the logo and branding designs for the new Moose Creek Film Festival. It's run by this big movie star, Cash Taylor. The guy from the *Never Die* series. It's going to be the next Sundance."

"That's wonderful, sweetie! You are just so talented."

"Thanks, mom. I'm really excited about it. Kelsey and her neighbor Derek are going to take me out to celebrate tonight."

"Oooh, Kelsey told me a little bit about this Derek guy. He sounds *very* cute."

"What?! Kelsey told you about him?" Kelsey was going to get an earful later.

"Of course, dear. Kelsey tells me everything." It *should* be sweet that Kelsey and my mom are so close. I did love that Kelsey was essentially my sister by this point in our lives. But I didn't need her telling my mom about Derek. "She said he likes you."

"Mom, stop. We're just friends."

She tutted on the other end of the phone. "That's not what it sounded like . . ."

"Well, Kelsey is a wishful thinker."

Mom let out a sigh and relented. "Congrats on your job, sweetie. That's really exciting; I'm so proud of you."

"Thanks, mom. That means a lot."

"I love you, honey. I've gotta hop off, though, or I'll be late to Teri's wake. It's going to be such a scene." I imagined her looking into her mirror, putting on her lipstick carefully, morbidly excited for the social event that would be Teri's wake.

I wanted to laugh but held back. "Love you, Mom."

The phone clicked off just as the snow began to fall. I tucked it under the towel and sat back, enjoying the winter wonderland of a scene playing out. Me, in the hot tub, enveloped in steam as a peaceful snow fell gently from the sky. It was a perfect Moose Creek afternoon.

Chapter 11

Kelsey stood in front of her closet; doors flung wide open. She rifled through the hangers like a secretary through a filing cabinet. Her face was pinched in concentration. Fashion was a serious business. Every few hangers she'd pause to consider a top or dress or skirt, her brows furrowed, shaking her head. I sat on the bed, watching in amusement as she muttered to herself under her breath.

"I think—"

"Shhh!" she hushed me sharply. She swiveled around to face me with a playful grin. "The artist is at work, madame."

"Désolée," I teased Kelsey back.

She returned to the task at hand, a woman on a mission. I had already decided on wearing my own clothes this evening: some vintage bell-bottom jeans and a snug black turtleneck, sans bra. I thought it was chic and sexy. Most importantly, it made *me* feel chic and sexy.

Kelsey pulled out a long silk slip dress in a striking shade of chartreuse that only someone as stunning as she could pull off. "Isn't that a little formal?" I asked, suddenly insecure in my casual outfit.

She shook her head, lips pursed. "Not at all. Wait till you see it styled." She looked at me thoughtfully before diving back into the closet. "I know *just* what to do." Of course, she did.

Kelsey grabbed a thin white turtleneck, not dissimilar to my black one, and placed it on the bed inside of the dress to denote it would be a layered look.

"Ooooh," I admired. "Very '90s."

"Mhmm." She grabbed a pair of white leather boots and set them down in front of the bed. "Yep, that's the look. And I'll wear my shearling coat over it. It'll still be casual, but very cute."

"Naturally." This routine of ours—Kelsey poring over her clothes and artfully putting together her outfit while I watched from the bed—had been happening since we were pre-teens. It was comforting in its familiarity. It reminded me that, no matter what, Kelsey and I would always be the same. At least to each other.

Kelsey got dressed quickly and looked incredible, as always. She was right—the dress was perfect. We touched up our makeup side-by-side in her master bathroom while Dina played with Noah downstairs.

"Here," Kelsey said, turning towards me, highlighter in hand. She swirled her fingers into the glittery cream and patted it into my cheekbones. "Just think you could use a little extra. This is a celebration, after all."

I admired myself in the mirror, my cheeks looking shiny and high, like sculpted glass. Looking closer, you could see the tiniest flecks of rose gold pigment. It was so pretty; I couldn't stop staring.

"You look hot," Kelsey said.

"So do you."

We both looked at ourselves in the mirror together. We *did* look hot. "Derek's going to die when he sees you."

"*Stop.*"

"He is! He'll be hiding an erection all night long, I bet," she teased.

"Yeah, because he'll have slept with half the bar probably."

"Oh, *you* stop it now! Who cares? Don't slut shame him."

"I'm not!"

"You kind of are," Kelsey said, looking thoughtful. "And how would you feel if someone said that about you or me, as a woman?"

"I'd say they were misogynists," I said, relenting. "Ugh, you're right."

"Of course, I am."

"I'm just bitter because he won't sleep with *me*."

"I know. But maybe that will change tonight! I can totally see your nips through that top. And it's sexy."

"Not too much?"

"Definitely not. You're wearing a turtleneck, after all. Gotta sex it up somehow," she joked.

"Right?" I agreed.

Derek arrived promptly at 7. Dina greeted him while Kelsey breast fed Noah on the couch. "You must be Derek," she said warmly.

"Yes, hello," he said as he came inside, his puffer coat was open, revealing a sliver of his outfit. He was wearing what appeared to be a buffalo-check flannel and slim cut black jeans. He looked cute, *too* cute.

"I'm Dina, darling. Come sit down. Kelsey's just feeding Noah before you kids head out." Dina radiated maternal energy and warmth. She was a smiley woman, tall and lithe like her daughter. Dina was calm and grounded, whereas my mom was gregarious and scatter-brained at times.

"Lovely to meet you Dina," Derek said with a smile as he sat down opposite Kelsey and me. Only Kelsey could make breastfeeding look so chic. "You ladies look amazing." He scanned our outfits. "Definitely the most fashionable women in Moose Creek."

"I don't know . . . Irina seemed to have some serious style," I teased.

Derek's face flushed slightly. "Ah, she's just superficial. That's not real style."

"Derek, where shall we go first this evening?" Kelsey asked.

"You know I'm always going to say Nell's . . ."

"How about something a little more . . . trendy? And then we can do Nell's after."

Derek shrugged. "Whatever you ladies want."

"Sounds great. If there's booze, I'm there!" I said, ready for the night to start.

"It's your night, babe," said Kelsey as she carried Noah into the kitchen to give to Dina.

It was just Derek and me now in the living room. He leaned forward in his seat, his eyebrows raised. "Seriously, Annie, you look amazing." His voice was hushed. It tickled the air and made it sound so much naughtier than it was. Like he was telling me a dirty secret. My stomach flipped as he ran his eyes over my body, lingering a moment too long on my lips and breasts.

I couldn't go there though. There was no way I was putting myself out there for a *third* time with Derek, only to get rejected again. For self-preservation's sake, I had to keep my own desire smooshed as far down as possible.

Kelsey strode in, her shearling coat now hooked onto her finger. I popped up from my seat, a little too eagerly. I couldn't handle Derek looking at me like that any longer, like he was going to devour me. If he wasn't going to sleep with me, *I* was no longer interested in him. No more cruel flirting and teasing me until I'm practically drooling and quivering uncontrollably.

The car service arrived promptly once Kelsey ordered it. "It's still on Rick's card," she smirked devilishly.

"Good. He owes you a lot more than a cab ride to the bar."

"Amen," cried out Dina from the kitchen. We all laughed.

Cramming into the backseat of the town car, I ended up in the tiny middle seat. Typical. "But you're the smallest," Kelsey would always whine whenever I tried to get her to take the middle seat back in the day. I don't think we'd been in the back-seat of a car like this together since she'd lived in New York.

Squished in the middle, I was uncomfortably aware of Derek's legs pushed up against mine. His taut, muscular legs felt so firm and warm against mine. He rested his hand casually on my thigh and my whole body seemed to swell. *Damn hormones.* He was like getting high from secondhand smoke. I didn't even have to take a toke from the joint. He filled the air, radiating sex, and my body just responded to it, whether I wanted it to or not. It was maddening. Clearly, I needed to get laid.

And if it wasn't going to be Derek, I'd just have to find someone tonight to do the job. It was the perfect opportunity. I looked hot, felt sexy, would have a couple drinks, and see what my options were. There were other sexy men in this town here for the slopes. Derek wasn't Moose Creek's only offering as far as hot men went. Maybe if I just had sex with someone, I'd be freed of my desire for Derek. I was probably just horny and lonely, or something.

The car dropped us off in front of The Peak, a cocktail bar that held prime real estate on Main Street. The golden glow from its windows beckoned us inside. Derek opened the door for us, like a gentleman, and we nestled into a booth. The bar was cozy and cabin-like, wood everywhere with plaid flannel cushions on the booths. Vintage Winter Olympics posters adorned the walls, while tealights were strewn about the tables and bar, casting the patrons in amber light.

Derek ordered from the bartender and brought us our drinks. Me, a dirty gin martini with extra olives, and Kelsey, a Manhattan. Derek, unsurprisingly, had a foaming pint of beer. He sat across from Kelsey and me and raised his glass high. "To Annie, the best damn graphic designer this side of the Mississippi."

"To Annie!" cried out Kelsey.

I snorted, but raised my glass to meet theirs, careful not to slosh any of my martini. "Thanks, you guys." I took a sip and let the cold briny taste dance on my tongue for a moment before swallowing.

"So does this mean you'll be sticking around Moose Creek for a while longer?" Derek sipped his beer, his voice casual, but Kelsey's eyes darted to mine. She arched her eyebrows suggestively, as if he meant anything other than polite conversation.

"I guess it does," I said with a nod. "At least through the opening of the festival. Then I have to get back to the city for a client that wants me on site for a project." I felt a pang of sadness in my chest at the thought of saying goodbye to Moose Creek. Never would I have expected how much this little ski town had come to mean to me. The longer I stayed, the more it felt like an extension of home . . . like a favorite old sweatshirt that's so soft and warm, you don't want to take it off. I was so much more relaxed here; I'd even ignored a few calls from clients back in New York. I wasn't attached to my phone and my email in Moose Creek, and I liked it.

"Good," Derek said softly. I cocked my head quizzically as I watched him drink his beer. He just smirked back, ever the tease. Was he hard to read or just a flirt? Moment to moment, my grasp of Derek changed. It was disorienting.

"Well, I'm certainly happy about that," chimed in Kelsey. She was grinning, her glossy lips shining in the candlelight. I saw her ten years younger then —wild and carefree, before Rick, before Noah. A pang of yearning hit me in the gut before evaporating with another sip of my martini. Those were fun years, single together in New York, making mistakes all over Manhattan, but I could honestly say that I was very content in this moment. Here, in Moose Creek, with my best friend Kelsey and my new friend Derek—my *very sexy* new friend Derek.

"I'm happy about it too. I love getting to see you every day again." I reached across the table and gave her hand a squeeze.

"Same . . . you know, Derek, Annie and I lived together in our early twenties. In the tiniest two-bedroom apartment on the Lower East Side."

"Our toilet was legit in a closet. The shower and sink were across the apartment. Which, to be fair, was only a few steps wide." I couldn't help but laugh remembering how dingy and cramped that apartment was, but how much we loved it. It was our first home as adult women, thriving in the big city. We felt like we were living the dream.

"And remember that neighbor who always played the saxophone at like 5am?!" Kelsey was laughing now, too.

Derek smiled, watching us reminisce. "Sorry," I said to him, worried he felt excluded. "I know we talk about the past a lot."

"No, please, continue. It's fun listening to you two like this . . . why did you leave New York, Kelsey?"

She let out a long exhale. "I followed a guy," she said, rolling her eyes. "I met Rick when he was on business in New York, and it felt like being struck by lightning. He was older, accomplished, cultured, he wined and dined me . . . he'd come to the city every few weeks and eventually, I fell in love. So, I moved out to Colorado to be closer to him. Got a job at Moose Creek Mountain in events. And then he wifed me up and decided I'd be better suited to being a trophy wife." She sighed heavily and took a sip of her cocktail. "Turns out, I wasn't. But I really, *really* tried to be." She looked down at her hands, eyeing her now empty ring finger, lips pursed.

"You were a good partner, Kels, and you're an incredible mother. He was a terrible husband—an absolute asshole, frankly." I nudged her, forcing her eyes to meet mine.

She smiled sadly. "I know . . . okay, enough of this bummer talk!" Lifting the stem of her glass, she downed the rest of her Manhattan. "Let's get *drunk!*"

"Impressive," said Derek.

"Next round is on me," said Kelsey, rising from the table.

Two martinis in and I was feeling good. It's amazing how the right amount of alcohol can make a night seem suddenly magical and full of possibilities. As we sat, joking and talking around the table, Derek's leg inched towards mine until it was outright touching me. I fought my instinct to move my leg away, as if he had accidentally bumped me, but he caught my gaze and held it. A faint smile creeped across his face as he gave me an almost imperceptible nod. Our legs stayed glued together and my pulse quickened as Kelsey vented about her coworkers.

"And then Yolanda looked me straight in the face and said—"

"Derek?!" A woman with wavy light brown hair strode over to our table, eyes lit up excitedly. "What a crazy coincidence running into you tonight . . ."

I shifted in my seat and my leg moved away from his ever so slightly. He glanced at me before landing on this unknown woman.

"Hey . . ." Derek smiled politely but I could see him racking his brain for her name.

"Jen," she said, her smile tightening. "From last year? You gave me lessons and . . . stuff . . . for like a week?" Jen searched Derek's face, hoping she'd jogged his memory successfully.

"Of course! Jen! Great to see you back in town this season," he said, his voice warm, as he nodded. If he didn't remember her, he was doing his best to play it off otherwise. Jen seemed satisfied with this, and her shoulders relaxed.

"Can't beat Moose Creek. Are you already all booked up or think you can squeeze me in some-time? I'll be here for a week." Her eyes narrowed as she bit her lip and leaned slightly forward, her cleavage dipping into better view. "I'm staying at The Evergreen again . . ."

I watched Derek carefully. Kelsey held her lips together, eyes bugging out wide, trying not to laugh awkwardly as her eyes darted between the two of them. Jen certainly wasn't being subtle about what squeezing her in meant. Part of me watched in amusement, while the other part tried to ignore the pang of jealousy I felt. She'd won Derek's affections in a way I hadn't, even if it was a year ago.

"Great!" he said brightly. "You can call the ski school tomorrow morning and see if I have any openings while you're here. I don't know my schedule offhand, but Shelby will be able to sort everything out for you."

Jen looked like she'd been slapped in the face. She took a step back and furrowed her brow. "Seriously?"

"Yes?" Derek's jaw tensed as he tried to remain calm, but his face was already beginning to flush.

"Derek, you fucked me for like a week straight last year. And you're really going to make me go through the ski school?"

His face was now fully red as he tried to diffuse the situation. "Um. I'm sorry, Jen. I thought we both had a fun time . . . but I really do only book ski lessons through the school's manager, Shelby."

"Wow." Jen straightened her back, her eyes dripping with disdain. She shook her head disapprovingly and turned on her heel, heading back to a few other women at the bar.

Kelsey burst into laughter. "*Wow*," she repeated, giggling uncontrollably. It was infectious; I began to lose it too. Then Derek finally chuckled, his face returning to its regular shade of tan.

"You're going to get some angry yelp reviews," I teased. "Some very dissatisfied customers . . . Irina, now Jen . . ."

"Oh, I don't think Derek has ever left a woman *dissatisfied*, Annie." Kelsey was now swiping away tears, trying to catch her breath between fits of laughter.

"Okay, okay . . . I know how it *looks*," said Derek.

"Oh, there's no way you can talk your way out of this," I said. "Remember Nina at Nell's? And then Irina? And now Jen! Derek, you are clearly the Casanova of Moose Creek, the Romeo of the Ski Runs, the Playboy of . . ."

"Pussy?" snorted Kelsey.

"Ah!" I squealed before dissolving into another fit of laughter.

Derek began to fidget with his almost empty

pint glass. "Okay, fine, I *did* have a bit of a reputation . . . but I'm not like that anymore."

"You've taken a vow of celibacy?" I asked solemnly.

He rolled his eyes and smirked. "No. I'm just not into having one-night stands and a string of casual flings with women who look at me like *that*." He tilted his head in Jen's direction, who kept sneaking scowling glances our way.

Kelsey and I quieted down. "I get that," she said. I just nodded, unsure of what to say. Unsure of how to feel.

"Let's get out of here." Derek finished his beer with a satisfied smile. "Time for Nell's." He got up and went to the bar to pay the tab, unbothered by Jen throwing daggers at him.

Kelsey ordered another car and we all piled in, chattering over each other on the short ride to Nell's Tavern. Nell welcomed us warmly from behind the bar.

A woman with dark curly hair piled atop her head was serving a couple guys that looked like Derek wannabes. She handed them their beers and walked over to us. "Derek, how are you, sweetie?"

"Hey Rita, I'm great. This is Kelsey. And Annie."

"Hi girls. What can I get you?"

We ordered a round of drinks and climbed into a booth. Kelsey began scanning the bar, landing on a group of fit guys in their thirties playing pool. She took a sip of her drink, eyeing them intently.

"They're cute." I nudged her with my elbow gently.

"They are . . . you know, I haven't had sex since Rick. Might be time to get back on the horse." She smirked mischievously. "Think I'll go say hello." She rose from the table, glass in hand, and sauntered over to the pool table, her blonde hair bouncing and her hips swaying confidently. The men paused their game, as if dumbfounded. She had that effect on men.

"Lucky guys," I mused, taking a sip of my drink.

"You really think they're cute?" Derek watched as the guys put down their pool cues and each began competing for Kelsey's attention.

"What, are you jealous?" I smirked and jutted my chin out defiantly.

"Maybe." He gave a sly smile as he studied my face.

"Well, you shouldn't be. You've made it pretty clear you aren't into me like that." I brought my drink to my lips and swallowed hard. I was too buzzed to care about being passive aggressive.

"What are you talking about, Annie?" He leaned in across the table, brow furrowed.

"Oh, don't play dumb with me, Derek."

He stared at me blankly. "I truly have no idea what you're talking about. How on earth have I given you the impression that I don't want you like that?"

My cheeks began to burn. "Are you kidding me?"

His eyes darted around my face, lost and pleading. He looked at me expectantly. "Annie . . ." His voice was hushed.

I couldn't help but soften as he bore into me with those pale blue eyes. "Each time I've put myself out there, you've rejected me. But you still manage to tease me and flirt with me—despite the fact that you don't actually want to sleep with me . . . A girl can only take so much! I've never considered myself fragile, but you've managed to really test me, Derek." I blinked back tears as I stared into my glass. It was humiliating, crying like this in the middle of a bar. To a guy that had rejected me multiple times over.

"Hey . . ." He got up and slid into the booth next to me. Gingerly tucking my hair behind my ear, he leaned in and kissed me. His warm hands cupped my face as he pressed his soft lips into mine.

"I never meant to hurt you, Annie," he said softly. He gently swiped my cheekbones, brushing my tears aside. "I thought I'd made it clear that with you, I want more than *just* sex, but obviously, I failed at that."

"What?" My voice wobbled slightly as I looked into his eyes, which were round and sincere.

"I *like* you, Annie . . . a lot."

"You do?"

He let out a soft chuckle and shook his head in disbelief. "Yes. I thought it was obvious."

"Why wouldn't you have sex with me? I thought you were dangling it above my head, like some cruel joke. Turning me on just to turn me down or something. I was so confused and frustrated."

He grabbed my hands and wrapped them in his, giving them a tight, reassuring squeeze. "I just didn't want this to be only a hookup thing . . ."

"But you sleep with everyone?" My mouth dropped open, immediately regretting having said that.

"All of that was just for fun. I didn't care about those women the way I do about you." He looked so serious.

My chest swelled and the room suddenly felt brighter, as if a heavy fog had cleared, and the sun was now shining. I'd told myself a story and believed it. But it hadn't been true. Derek *liked* me. Before I could second guess myself, I wrapped my arms around him and kissed him hard, running my hands through that shaggy mop of hair. He pulled me into his lap, right there on the booth, in the middle of Nell's Tavern, and kissed me passionately.

Cheers rang out from the pool table, and we began to laugh into each other's mouths. We reluctantly pulled apart to see Kelsey holding up a pool cue triumphantly. Her face was spread wide in a smile, watching us, as she whooped and hollered. The men clustered around her echoed her. I giggled awkwardly and leaned into Derek, our foreheads pressed together.

"These are on the house." Nell dropped two flutes of cheap champagne on the table. "About time you got yourself a girl, Derek. She seems like a good one."

"She is." He nodded and gave my waist a covert squeeze. My stomach did somersaults as we toasted each other. The sweet bubbles trickled down my throat and my cheeks began to ache from smiling. What was happening? This all felt like a dream, and I didn't want to wake up anytime soon.

Chapter 12

I was so turned on that I couldn't even feel the freezing cold as I stood on Derek's front porch. We stumbled through the door, our limbs tangled around each other. He unzipped my coat and tossed it aside, not bothering to hang it up. I tugged at his jacket eagerly and he peeled it off as Coyote nudged us impatiently with his nose.

"Not now, Coyote," muttered Derek, absent-mindedly petting the top of his head with one hand, the other gripping my waist. Without taking his lips off me, he steered me toward the staircase. He spun me around and grabbed my ass, giving it a firm squeeze. "I'm gonna grab Coyote a bone so he doesn't bother us." He disappeared into the kitchen, and I quickly run my hands through my hair, smoothing it down.

I swiped under my eyes, trying to remove any mascara that may have smeared. Derek reappeared and tossed Coyote his bone. With a wag of his tail, he caught the bone and hopped onto the couch with it, ready to chew.

"Now, where were we?" Derek leaned in and kissed me, cradling my head in his hands, before leading me upstairs. At the top of the landing, he spun me around to face him and pushed my back up against the wall. I let out an excited gasp as he pressed his body into mine. The weight of him against me, pinning me to the wall, was over-whelming—in the best way. I couldn't help but roll my hips against him, begging for more. We kissed deeply; our tongues entangled in each other's mouths.

"I've wanted to do this since we first met," he whispered as he skated his hands up my body and began to rub my nipples with his thumb, gripping my breasts in his palms. They shrunk and stiffened at his touch as my heartbeat echoed between my legs. "They were staring at me all night, begging to be touched." He nibbled my earlobe as he gently pinched them. I knew I was dripping wet already.

"You were staring at my tits all night? . . . Naughty boy . . ." I moved my hands down to his ass, giving him a playful spank. He pinched my nipples harder in response. I gasped, electricity surging through my body.

"How could I not? In that thin little turtleneck, without a bra? I was at risk of a hard-on all night."

"Really?" I giggled, pleased at the thought. Maybe I had more power over him than I had thought . . . and here I'd thought he'd held it all.

"Uh-huh," he grunted, his hands now on my ass. He gripped me hard, pulling me into him tightly. I could feel how hard he was underneath his jeans.

"Mmmm . . ." I moaned softly and grinded my hips against him, letting his thickness rub against me. He threaded his hands around my waist and hoisted me up. I wrapped my legs around him as our kissing became sloppier and heavier. I wanted to taste every inch of him.

Derek carried me into his bedroom and threw me down on his bed. An excited squeal escaped my lips as he hovered over me, eyes darkened with lust. I glanced down to see his cock straining against his jeans, the bulge begging to be let free. Reaching towards him, I trailed my fingertips teasingly against it, and he grunted before diving in to kiss me hungrily.

We made out on his bed, our hands running over every inch of each other, grabbing greedy handfuls of whatever we could. I writhed against him, feeling the ache inside me grow. I needed him; I was becoming desperate. His lips curled into a lazy smirk as I looked up at him pleadingly and fumbled with the hem of his shirt. He yanked it off, tossing it aside, before slowly peeling my turtleneck up over my head.

With every new bit of skin revealed, he kissed and licked me. He ran his tongue up over my breasts, sucking and nibbling on each one, refusing to rush. I moaned as he savored every inch of my skin. When he finally pulled my top completely off, he took in a sharp inhale, as if trying to steady himself. His pale blue eyes were glazed over in wanting as they glided over my naked chest.

"You are so beautiful, Annie." His voice was low and thick. Just the sound of it made my skin tingle.

"Come here," I whispered, reaching my arms out to him. I ran my palms over the ripples of his chest and abdomen, letting the ridges of muscle rise and fall beneath them. I swiped at his sides, trying to grip his strong waist, beckoning his body to mine.

His skin was hot against mine as I pressed my breasts into him, caressing his neck with my lips and grazing my teeth along his broad shoulders. He groaned and knotted his hands in my hair, which had become wild and untamed in the throes of passion. Tugging gently, he pulled my face to his and kissed me hard before pushing me back against the bed. He laid me down and hovered above me, looking like a lion about to devour his prey. It sent a thrill down my spine as my heartbeat thundered inside me. Desire rattled inside me like a caged animal, clawing to be free.

"Please," I begged, my body squirming, desperate to be touched and kissed more.

He gave a sly smile—that boyish grin was now a very manly smirk. "I'm gonna take my time with you." Gripping my hips in one hand, he unzipped my jeans with the other and slid them off my body. I laid on the bed in nothing but a red lace thong. His eyes feasted on me as his hands held me still. God, I wanted him to touch just a bit lower . . .

Tracing his fingers along the lace of my underwear, his breathing became ragged. "Jesus Christ, Annie," he muttered, his voice raspy.

"Derek," I whispered.

We locked eyes, and his hand slid underneath my thong. I gasped softly as he drew circles over my clit. My back arched as my hips pushed into his hand, wanting more. He slid his hand lower, to my opening, and moaned. "You're so wet," he rasped.

I rocked my hips towards him, and he gently teased me open, coaxing me with his forefinger until he could slip another one inside. I groaned when he found my g-spot and began to stroke while his thumb rubbed my clit. His mouth fell open as he watched me writhe in pleasure from his touch. I whimpered as the pressure mounted inside me.

He licked his lips and pried my legs farther apart as he shimmied down the bed and began to kiss my inner thigh. He dragged his tongue up my thigh and onto my pussy. I gasped and my whole body shivered. "Derek," I panted. Tracing my nails across his scalp, I threaded my fingers through his thick blonde hair as he pressed his tongue into me. He licked and nibbled and kissed, sucked and circled and massaged.

My body felt like it was compressing. I was panting, and sweat had begun to cling to my lower back as my hips bucked up uncontrollably against him. He gripped me, digging into my hip with one hand to steady me, as he stroked faster and licked harder until I burst. A howl escaped my lips as I came hard, seeing colors explode behind my eyes, my breath loud and ragged, my eyes watery.

Derek smiled above me, satisfied with himself, his eyes still glazed over in that turned on way. He slowly circled my clit now, his fingers slippery from me. My body shivered at how good it still felt as I tried to catch my breath.

"How . . . how did you do that?" I asked in between breaths, feeling like I had been transported to another dimension. I'd never had a man give me an orgasm like that.

He didn't answer, he just grinned and kissed me. "I love seeing you wild like that."

"I want to make you go wild, too."

He grabbed a lock of my hair and twirled it around his finger. "You already make me go wild."

I trailed my hand down his body and brushed it over the front of his pants. He was still hard. I twisted the button and unzipped; his erection sprung free, tenting his boxers. "See?" he asked, his breathing turning shallow, as I tugged his underwear and pants off.

I carefully wrapped my fingers around him, and we both let out a gasp. I loved feeling him stiff and ready in my hand; I wanted to taste him. Pressing my lips into his neck, I kissed my way down his body. His skin was salty and warm. I ran my fingers through the tuft of hair above his thick cock and then began to lick him slowly and teasingly.

He moaned. "Annie . . ." It just spurred me on, hearing him say my name, his voice ragged. But I didn't want to give in just yet. I ran my tongue along his shaft and swirled it around the tip. He grunted as he watched me, eyes half closed. When I finally took him in my mouth, he gasped loudly, "Fuck!"

I smiled against his cock as I moved up and down until he was trembling uncontrollably and muttering incoherently. I felt so powerful.

"Annie, please," he panted. "I need to be inside of you."

I grinned, my cheeks flushed, and crawled up to him. He kissed me hungrily, passion surging between us like an electrical storm. He wrapped his arms around me tightly and swiveled me around so he could enter me. I held onto his broad, freckled shoulders as he pushed into me.

We both gasped, locking eyes, as our bodies melted into one another. He filled my body and warmth spread through me, my skin tingling and my ears buzzing. He plunged inside me, and I wrapped my arms around him tightly, drawing him as close as I could.

We kissed, our tongues tangling, as my hips bucked against him. My body writhed and undu-lated, against my will. I couldn't control my move-ments; I was coming undone. I moaned and gasped, my eyes rolling back in my head. Every stroke felt like it would tip me over the edge. My thighs convulsed as wave after wave of pleasure moved through my body. He whispered my name in low, raspy breaths, "Annie, Annie, Annie," as if he was praying to me.

"Don't stop," I demanded, desperate to somehow get closer, deeper than we already were. My vision blurred and my body shook as I came.

Derek was panting and sweaty, his face contorting, and he quickly pulled out, his own orgasm falling onto my bare thigh with a heavy thud. I watched in awe as he came, swelling and then falling onto me. Our ragged breaths filled the air as we laid side by side in bed.

"Come here," he whispered, pulling me into him.

"I'm all messy," I said apologetically.

"I don't care." He wrapped his arms around me and held me closely. I rested my head on his chest, letting his light smattering of chest hair tickle my cheek.

"I see why you have so many women throwing themselves at you." My breathing began to slow and return to normal. I could hear his heartbeat, steady and strong, underneath my ear, reverberating in his chest.

He raised his head and looked at me, wincing. "Don't say that."

"What?"

"It's not like that with other women. I don't make love to them."

My cheeks burned. *Make love?* "Oh . . ."

"I mean it, Annie. I *like* you . . . more than just like you, really."

I raised my head and propped up onto my side, facing him. "You do?"

He turned over and looked at me, then gently kissed me on the forehead. "Yes, I do."

I leaned back into him and let him hold me until my eyes were so heavy and my body so tired that I fell asleep.

A LOUD KNOCK THUNDERED THROUGH THE HOUSE, startling me awake. It took a second for me to get my bearings. I wasn't in Kelsey's guest bedroom, and I wasn't alone.

Derek grunted, groggy.

"Who's knocking on your door?" I yawned into my pillow as Derek ran his fingertips up my arm lazily.

Another knock echoed out from downstairs. Derek groaned, kissed my forehead, and stumbled to his feet, rubbing his eyes. He tugged on his boxers and grumbled as he made his way downstairs.

I sighed, rolling over, ready to fall back asleep. I heard the door swing open downstairs. And then heard what sounded like Kelsey's voice and Noah squealing. Scanning his room, I saw a sweatshirt draped over an armchair in the corner and grabbed it. I pulled it on over my head and padded downstairs.

"Hey sleepyhead," Kelsey called out. She grinned knowingly. "Looks like you had a busy night." Noah squealed and flailed his arms as Kelsey held him.

"Hey," I croaked.

"I have to go into work earlier than planned. Cash scheduled a last-minute meeting with the events team."

"We're gonna watch Noah," Derek said, holding his hand out to Noah. He grabbed his forefinger with his tiny fist and shook it.

"Sorry, I know it's not the sexiest way to spend a morning." Kelsey glanced at me, apologetic. "But Dina's able to pick him up in a few hours."

"Ah don't worry about," Derek said. Noah lunged for him, and Derek scooped him up in his arms. He spun him around like a helicopter, and Noah giggled maniacally.

Kelsey winked at me, eyebrows raised, before

getting up. "Well, Noah seems to be a big fan of Derek's already."

I smiled, watching them. "He does."

Derek chuckled as Noah grabbed a fistful of Derek's shaggy hair and pulled. "Hey little man, don't go pulling my hair out." Noah cackled.

"Call me if you need anything," Kelsey said from the doorway. "Thanks again!"

"Bye!" Derek called out as he began tossing and catching Noah. Coyote watched, tail wagging. Derek was such a natural with Noah.

"Should I make some coffee?" I offered.

"I can do it for us. Wanna hold onto this little guy?"

I took Noah into my arms and kissed his little cheeks as he beamed up at me. He babbled away on my hip as I watched Derek make coffee, whistling to himself. His boxers clung to his pert, muscular behind. I hoped I'd get to grab a handful again sometime soon. I still couldn't believe how good the sex was last night. From his reputation around Moose Creek, I assumed he would be a skilled lover, but that had been mind-blowing—and more passionate than any sex I'd ever had.

Derek handed me my coffee as I held onto Noah with one arm. I blew on the steam and took the tiniest sip. "You remembered how I like my coffee."

That boyish grin again. "Of course. Creamy with a little bit of sugar." He gave my ass a little squeeze and kissed my cheek. "You look good with a baby on your hip."

"Well, that's just because he's being a little angel right now." I kissed the top of Noah's head, thankful he was being so easy.

"Do you want kids?"

"What?!" I had not expected that question.

Derek laughed and sat down at the kitchen table with his mug of coffee. "Does that question freak you out?"

"Um . . ." I sat down across from him, unsure of what to say, as I propped Noah up on my lap. His little hands slapped the table excitedly. "I think so . . . with the right person."

"I've been told I'd make an excellent father." He jutted his chin out and smirked before taking a sip of coffee.

"So, you definitely want kids then?"

"Yeah, I want to have a family. For sure."

"Hm," I murmured, nodding. Derek watched me, his head to cocked to the side. "What?"

"Are you surprised?" he asked.

"I mean, you're great with Noah, but you don't

really act like someone who's looking for something serious and is ready to start a family." I shrugged awkwardly.

"What? Because I've slept around? Because I'm just a ski bum?" His voice sounded wounded.

My heart sank to my stomach, and I winced. "The sleeping around . . ."

Derek frowned. "Maybe I just hadn't met the right woman yet."

"The benefit of being a man, I guess. You don't have to worry about your biological clock ticking away, warning you that your time is limited. You can take your time and have all the fun you want."

Derek's pale eyes searched my face, his brow furrowed. I felt exposed and my face began to get hot. Noah slammed his hands down on the table and began to wail. I'd spoken too soon about him being an angel. "Hey, hey," I said soothingly, bouncing my knee. He screamed louder. "What's wrong, baby boy?" I stood up and turned him around. His face was scrunched up and dripping fat tears.

Swaying from side to side, I tried rocking him, but he continued crying. With every second, he only got louder and angrier. I checked his diaper, peeking inside only to find it still clean. The wails were unbearable. "Please stop, please stop," I begged, jostling my hip, trying to quell him.

"Let me try," Derek said, holding out his arms. I handed Noah to him as he screeched into the air. Derek didn't flinch, though. He continued to bounce him. "It's okay, little man," he said reassuringly. He began twirling around with him slowly, until the wails turned to sniffles. I watched in awe as Noah quieted down. Derek spun him faster until Noah burst into the giggles, his damp face spread wide into a smile now.

"Wow," I said with a sigh of relief. "I'm impressed."

He shrugged cutely and grinned.

My chest swelled as I watched him play with Noah. "You really are going to be a great father."

"Told you," he said with a wink.

Chapter 13

THAT NIGHT, I FELT LIKE I HAD WHIPLASH AS I headed to my dinner with Cash. I'd just had incredible sex with Derek and couldn't stop thinking about him, but now I was having dinner with a huge movie star. *Was this really my life now?*

Cash rose from the table as I crossed the restaurant. A few patrons at their tables huddled together, whispering while they snuck covert glances at him—and now, me. I wondered if this happened everywhere he went and if it made him uncomfortable. Or maybe there was a small bit of him that enjoyed it, that got high off the attention, and liked feeling important. He was a famous movie star, after all.

"Annie, hi!" He grinned, those perfect white teeth sparkling in the dim light of the restaurant.

I reached out my hand and he shook it firmly,

his dark, round eyes locked on mine. "You look beautiful."

"Thanks . . . I hope I'm not underdressed." I glanced at his well-tailored suit and then down at my jeans and vintage silk blouse. I'd picked out a top that I thought was sophisticated and classy— soft, flowing crimson silk that was a little oversized for me, but in a chic way I thought. But now I realized, I should have put on a dress, or at least a blazer.

"Not at all," he said, motioning for me to sit down. "You're perfect."

I sat down and place the white linen napkin in my lap, trying to remember the table manners my mother had taught me when I was little. There were so many utensils on the table. Why did I need this many forks? A server immediately appeared, pouring me a glass of water. He and Cash exchanged a knowing nod.

"I hope you don't mind I already ordered us a bottle of wine." The server came back with an expensive-looking bottle of French wine. I'm sure I'd never even tasted something so fancy. For all I knew, it costed more than my rent. He uncorked it gently and poured a taste for Cash, who nodded approvingly.

"Is anyone else joining us from the team?"

There were still two empty chairs, albeit they didn't have place settings.

"No, I was hoping we could spend some time together, just the two of us, if that's all right." He smiled and took a sip of his wine.

"Of course." I brought the ruby-colored wine to my mouth and sipped carefully. It tasted as expensive as it looked—bright but complex while still being what I'd call 'easy-to-drink.' "Wow . . . that's delicious."

"I'm so glad you like it. I know not everyone would be pleased that their date just ordered a bottle of wine for them without asking." He let out a chuffed chuckle. *Date?* I felt a pang of nervous of energy flutter in my stomach, followed by a sting of guilt as I thought of Derek inside of me the night before, his lips on my skin and hands gripping me tightly.

I forced a smile, trying to hide how awkward I was feeling. "Well, you have great taste . . . have you eaten here before?"

He nodded. "Too many times, I'm afraid. Everything they do is delicious. The chef is a wizard."

I studied the menu, unsure of what to order. "So, you can't recommend anything in particular? It all looks so good . . ."

Cash let out a charming laugh. "How about we split a few things? Why limit ourselves?"

He ordered us a feast—caviar, burrata, surf and turf, branzino, an array of sides. It was too much, but Cash took mouthfuls of every dish. His eyes closed in bliss as he chewed, nodding approvingly. And he was right—everything was delicious. I'd never had such a decadent meal; each bite was richer and tastier than the previous.

We made typical, polite small talk, getting to know each other. Cash grew up in Ohio, the youngest of three kids. His mom was a nurse, dad was an electrician. He'd started acting in school plays and then moved out to Los Angeles after high school to start modeling. That took off and then he did a little soap acting until he started getting cast in larger parts in movies and finally, he won the part of the debonair spy, Benjamin Daniels, in the *Never Die* movies. The third of which was set to film in Sicily that summer.

I felt so uncool talking about myself, but he laughed at my jokes and smiled intently as I spoke. He listened closely, eyes dancing around my face. His attention was warm and exciting, but I kept thinking about Derek in the back of mind. I was, apparently, on a date with one of the hottest actors in the zeitgeist—any woman would die to be in my position. And yet, I couldn't stop picturing Derek's boyish grin, the slope of his freckled nose, his wild mop of sun-bleached hair. He'd look ridiculous in a fancy restaurant like this. I didn't even know if he owned a suit. And, you know what . . . I realized I really didn't care. A yearning for him began to bubble inside me. I tried to ignore it by drinking more wine and asking Cash questions about himself, but my attention drifted farther away the longer I sat there with him.

I still wasn't sure what last night had meant to Derek . . . was it just scratching a sexual itch? He said he liked me, and I *certainly* liked him, but he was such a flirt. A self-admitted playboy. And can a man like that really change? Plus, we didn't even live in the same state. How could it really be anything more than sex? Was I just setting myself up for heartbreak . . . *again*?

"Would you agree with that?"

"Huh?"

Cash looked at me expectantly. "That the resort is ready for the festival?"

"Oh, yes, definitely." I nodded reassuringly, trying to hide the fact that I hadn't been paying attention. "I know it's coming up quickly, but everyone's working so hard on it. It's going to be great."

He smiled, pleased. "I think so too."

After Cash insisted on ordering us a dessert to share—the best crème brûlée I'd ever tasted—he offered me a ride home in his town car. In the backseat, we chatted as the driver took us back to Kelsey's house.

"I had a lovely evening with you," he said.

"I did too. Thank you so much for dinner. It was truly fantastic."

He held my gaze intensely. *Was he expecting me to kiss him?* Before I could overthink it, I leaned in and pressed my lips against his, and waited for the butterflies to flap their wings inside me. I didn't feel anything. When Derek kissed me, I felt overwhelmed, as if my heart might fall out of my body or I might pass out from how much I wanted him.

Cash pulled away from me, almost bristling. "I'm so sorry, Annie, I think you misunderstood me tonight."

My face reddened. "What? Was this not a date? You said the word date when you picked out the wine!" I was frantically trying to regain my dignity, but it was quickly slipping away.

"Oh, I'm so sorry, I really didn't mean it like that . . . you are a *great* girl, though."

I stared at him blankly as he smiled apologetically. I only kissed him in the first place in hopes it would drive Derek out of my mind, and it had completely failed to do so.

"Oh, okay, I understand." I shifted awkwardly in my seat, wishing I was anywhere else in the world.

"Uh, well, I actually . . . really like your friend Kelsey. I was hoping . . . you could help me out with her."

I looked up at him. He looked nervous to admit this, but I was suddenly *thrilled*. It erased all my embarrassment from trying to kiss him a moment before. Cash would be *perfect* for Kelsey! And she was already enamored with him before she had ever even met him thanks to his *Never Die* movies. "Really?! That's wonderful!"

Cash looked taken aback, his mouth slightly parted. "It is?"

"Yes!" I nodded furiously.

"But you just tried to kiss me?"

"Forget about that! I was confused, I'm sorry . . . but I think you should absolutely ask Kelsey out on a date. She would have *loved* that restaurant."

His eyes lit up. "Yeah?" I nodded. "So, she doesn't have some cool snowboarder boyfriend?"

I laughed. "She does not. She's a single pringle. Very ready to mingle. With you."

He smiled to himself sweetly. "Well, I'll have to

do something about that then . . ."

The car pulled up in front of the townhouse, and I gave Cash an enthusiastic peck on the cheek. "Thank you again for tonight!"

He chuckled. "Anytime, Annie. Have a good night." He cocked his chin and flashed another megawatt smile. With a smile and a nod goodbye, I slipped out of the car and hurried through the cold night air.

"Hiiii," I trilled, swinging the door open, beaming with excitement. I couldn't wait to tell Kelsey that her crush, Hollywood hunk Cash Taylor *liked* her. She was going to flip.

"Hey." It was Derek. He was sitting with Noah and Kelsey on the couch. A fire was crackling in the fireplace as Noah slept in Kelsey's arms.

"Oh. Hi." I glanced at Kelsey awkwardly.

"Derek just stopped by to bring you some flowers." She nodded towards to the coffee table. A tall vase of bursting orange tulips sat atop it. "And he ended up building us a nice fire." Kelsey smiled tightly and raised her eyebrows.

"Those are for me?" I dropped my bag in the armchair and picked the vase up, admiring the flowers. Lee never brought me flowers like this . . . Come to think of it, I don't think any man had ever given me flowers before. "They're beautiful."

"I read somewhere that orange was the color of passion." Derek tilted his chin up at me, studying my face. "How was your date?"

Guilt churned in my stomach, and I thought I might be sick. "It wasn't a date." I sat down quietly, unable to look at him for too long.

"I'm gonna go put Noah to bed," Kelsey said in a hushed voice, excusing herself.

"Annie, why didn't you tell me you were getting dinner with Cash Taylor tonight?"

"I didn't know it was a big deal."

"We spent the night together last night . . . and then you went out with another man."

"Cash had wanted to take me out as a congratulatory thing, like for booking the gig. *I swear*, it wasn't a date."

"Of course, it was a date, Annie. Any man would fall over himself just to take you out." Derek rubbed his jaw, frustrated.

"What?" He was being ridiculous. Who did he think I was? Kelsey was the one who men fawned over, not me. "Derek, it really wasn't a big deal," I insisted. I didn't want to tell Derek about Cash's feelings for Kelsey until I'd had the chance to spill the tea to her first.

His pale blue eyes searched my face. "Last night meant something to me. I thought it did to you, too." *Ouch.* He looked so wounded, his broad shoulders hunched over as he held his jaw in his hands.

"It did." I got up and stood in front him, tipping his chin up to look at me. "Hey," I whispered. "It meant something to me, too."

Derek sighed and grabbed the back of my thighs, pulling me closer to him as he sank his face into my stomach. I ran my fingers through his shaggy hair as he rubbed the backs of my legs.

"I'm sorry about tonight . . . I promise it *was not* a date. And I couldn't stop thinking about you anyway."

"Really?" He looked up at me. I nodded. "Good," he said with a smile. "I want to be the one to take you out to dinner."

"Okay, then . . ."

"You'll let me?"

I sighed, trying to let go of my doubts and fear. Maybe his old playboy ways were latent, lying dormant just to come back to life with a vengeance, but maybe he really was reformed. He said he liked me, and why should I deny myself this chance at happiness? "Yeah." I nodded and smiled slyly. "I'll let you."

Derek stood up and grabbed me firmly, the feeling of his body up against mine sent a thrill down my spine. He kissed me hard, and I wrapped my arms around him, feeling the tight muscles in his back. I melted into him. I never wanted to stop kissing him or touching him.

"Let's go upstairs," I whispered, taking his hand, and leading him to the guest bedroom.

I delicately closed the door and spun around. Derek's eyes were on me, dark and hungry. I stepped to him, and he curled his hand around my waist. He skated his other hand up, over my shoulder, along my collarbone, and to my jaw. He held my head and brushed his thumb against my lip, lightly at first. Then he pressed it firmly, and I parted my lips. His thumb slipped inside my mouth, and I sucked as I stared up into the deep blue wells of his eyes. He bit his lip and grunted. I grazed my teeth against his thumb as he withdrew it from my mouth slowly.

Gripping my waist harder, he steered me towards the bed, pushing me to its edge. "Sit." I did as I was told, and he knelt before me. He grabbed each leg and unzipped my boots, casting them aside carelessly. His eyes stayed locked on mine. He slid his open palms greedily up my legs, fingers splayed wide. He undid my pants, yanking them down and off my legs, taking my underwear with them.

I sat there, naked and exposed, except for my red silk blouse. Heat flowed through my body as my desire for Derek swelled. His eyes danced over my body and landed between my legs. It was obscene the way he looked at me—like he was starving, and I was the only thing that could satisfy him. My skin was humming, and my ears were ringing. I wanted him so badly.

He trailed his fingers along my bare thighs and pushed them apart, spreading me open like a fan. I gasped, excited, as he dug his hands into the creases of my hips, holding me steady as he began to taste me. He teased my opening with his tongue, drawing circles and shapes I couldn't make out. My eyes rolled back in my head as I squirmed, pleasure coursing through my veins.

"Fuck," I panted, my hands grabbing fistfuls of the duvet underneath me. I twisted them tightly as my breath hitched. Derek's mouth was cracking me open. Every part of me spilled out; I could not be contained.

"I want to do this every day," he groaned into me. He dove his tongue inside me, flicking it hard. "Fuck, Annie. You taste so good." His breath was ragged, his voice thick and dark. It pushed me over the edge.

I rolled my hips against his mouth, riding his tongue to orgasm. A loud cry escaped my lips, and I quickly clapped my hand over my mouth, remembering we weren't alone in the house. Derek didn't care, he kept tasting me.

"I want you inside me," I panted, reaching down, and grasping at his elbows. "I need it." I tugged on his arms, pulling him up off his knees. Kissing him desperately, as if I was running out of time, I peeled off his shirt. I clawed at his pants, fumbling with the button.

Derek let out a low laugh and yanked them off for me. I caught the hem of my shirt and pulled it off over my head before pushing his boxers down over his erection. He sprung free, hard and throbbing. My mouth watered at the sight. He scooped me up, propping me up further on the bed, and kissed me, deep and slowly. Our tongues tumbled in and out of each other's mouths as I grabbed at his muscly ass, trying to pull him inside me. He slowly pushed himself in; we both sighed. God, it felt so good. I melted like a puddle into him as our bodies rocked against each other. Our rhythm was slow as we sank into each other deeply, moving like ocean tides.

My back arched as I held onto his shoulders, which were broad and rigid with muscle beneath my hands. With deft arms, he lifted my hips as my legs wrapped around his waist and flipped us over. I straddled him, grinding my ass against him, thrusting him as deeply inside as I could. He groaned, his hands gripping my ass. His fingers dug into the soft flesh, and I moaned. I rode him, my hands bracing myself on his taut chest.

"God, you feel unbelievable, Annie," he rasped. His hands traced the curves of my body, over my hips, dipping into my waist, and up to my breasts. He cupped them and grunted. My nipples stiffened like small cherry gumdrops as he massaged me, gently at first, but rougher and more desperate as I began to rock my hips faster against him.

With every thrust, we grunted and moaned, our panting now synchronized. The pressure was mounting inside me; I felt like a balloon ready to pop. I trembled as I came, ecstasy washing over me as Derek unraveled beneath my thighs, a series of swears escaping his lips. I collapsed on top of him, exhausted but blissed out.

He was damp with sweat, but I liked the way he smelled, like firewood left out in the rain mixed with musk. I buried my face into his chest, breathing him in as my lips brushed against his skin. *Was this love or was I just overwhelmed by lust and carnal pleasure?* Derek's breathing slowed as he rubbed my back sweetly. We were quiet. There wasn't anything to say that hadn't already been said with our bodies.

Chapter 14

I woke up the next morning to an empty bed. The only sign that Derek had been there the night before was my rumpled sheets. I pressed my face into his pillow and inhaled. It still smelled like him, so I know it hadn't been just a very good dream. I checked my phone to see if he had texted me but didn't have any messages. Had he just left me without saying goodbye? A familiar sinking feeling in the pit of my stomach grew.

The last night I'd spent with Lee, he'd left early in the morning. My memory of it is hazy as I was half asleep when he'd crawled out of bed and kissed my cheek goodbye, saying he had an early meeting at work. It wasn't unusual and he wasn't acting strange, so I had just rolled over and gone back to sleep, thinking nothing of it. But then I never saw him again. Never heard from him again. My texts to him went unanswered. So did my calls. And my instant messages on social media. I redownloaded the dating app we'd met on and he'd unmatched with me, his profile gone. It was torturous and heartbreaking, and to this day, I still don't know why he'd disappeared.

I glanced around the room, looking for anything Derek could have left as an indicator he'd be back. His clothes were all gone. There wasn't a note. I listened carefully to the quiet sounds of the house, hoping he had just gone to the bathroom or was downstairs helping himself to breakfast. The silence burned my ears and a wave a nausea rushed over my body. I couldn't go through this pain again; I can't believe I thought Derek might be different.

Running my hands through my hair, I steeled myself for the possibility that he had made a mistake—that I'd made a mistake. For all I knew, we'd both regret the last forty-eight hours. The one small mercy was that Derek lived next door, so he couldn't totally vanish. I'd at least know he hadn't died in a freak accident, which is what I'd grimly hoped for with Lee's ghosting at one low point.

I dragged myself out of bed, wrapping my soft, fuzzy robe around me for warmth, and padded downstairs. Kelsey was eating yogurt as Noah crushed handfuls of cereal in his highchair. She looked up and grinned knowingly. "Long night?"

Shaking my head, I plopped down on the chair next to her. "He left." I frowned, unable to hide my hurt.

"What are you talking about?"

"I woke up, and he was gone. I don't know what time he left, but he certainly didn't stick around or say goodbye. No text. No note . . . just poof! Gone."

"Annie, he just ran out to the store to get more coffee. We were out."

"Really?" I was shocked, but I probably shouldn't have been. Of course, I'd assumed the worst . . .

Kelsey chuckled softly. "Yes, really. He didn't want to wake you—said you were sound asleep."

"Oh." My face cracked open into a smile, and the tightness in my chest dissipated. I let out a long exhale of relief. "I was so convinced he'd made a run for it," I said, shaking my head.

"Annie, he wouldn't do that! He's crazy about you."

"I mean, that's what I thought about Lee . . ."

"Fuck Lee! He was a selfish, scared little prick."

I let out a small laugh and nodded. "Yeah . . ."

"And has Derek given you any reason to doubt his character?"

"Not directly, no . . . but all those other women! He's clearly a ladies' man. Maybe I'm just a passing fancy." I held my face in my hands and groaned. "I hate that I like him so much."

Kelsey elbowed me playfully and leaned in. "You are not just a passing fancy. Trust me."

"You don't know that."

"Oh, but I do . . ." she raised her eyebrows dramatically. "When Derek brought those flowers over last night, he let slip that you're the first woman he's felt like this about in *years*."

"Really?" My heart swelled in my chest.

Kelsey nodded seriously. "Yep."

"Huh." I bit my bottom lip, mulling this revelation over. "But years for a guy who's been having nonstop sex with whomever he pleases might not mean that much. Like, feeling more than what? More than he's felt for his one-night stands?"

"*Annie.*" Kelsey shook her head, frustrated with me. "Stop trying to convince yourself that he doesn't like you, that this doesn't mean something. I've seen you two together, and I know you better than I know myself . . . what's between you two is real."

I sighed. She was right; I was weaving a story with a bad ending. In my gut, I knew that our connection wasn't like what I'd had with Lee, or any of the guys before him. And when Derek looked at me, when he touched me, when he kissed me, I knew he felt the same way. I was so afraid of getting hurt, of being cast aside and abandoned, that I didn't want to accept it.

"It's going to be fine," Kelsey said, squeezing my hand reassuringly, as a knock suddenly sounded from the front door.

I nodded, rising to my feet. I went to the front of the townhouse and opened the door slowly, a surprising rush of nerves bubbling up inside me.

"You're awake," Derek said, flashing that boyish grin. At the sight of it, my stomach somersaulted.

"I am. I thought you'd left." I laid it out on the table, not bothering trying to play it cool.

Derek came inside, his face falling. "Oh, Annie, no. I would never just leave you." He set down the grocery bag and wrapped his arms around me tight, brushing the hair out of my face and kissing my forehead. "I woke up early and saw you were out of coffee."

"I know, Kelsey told me." He was being so sweet and reassuring, I started to cry. All my fears surfaced in big wet tears. "I'm just so afraid you're going to disappear or change your mind about me."

He held me tighter. "I'm not going anywhere. As long as you'll have me, I'm yours." His lips brushed against my forehead again. I tipped my chin up, looking up at him from his chest, his arms still wound tightly around me. He kissed each of my tearstained cheeks and then my lips.

I kissed him deeply and then laughed into his mouth. "I'm such an idiot. Working myself up like this."

"Well, you're my idiot now." Derek smirked and gave me another kiss. I was more than happy to be *his* idiot.

I LET DEREK CONVINCE ME TO GO SKIING WITH HIM that afternoon. Despite the nerves that enveloped me at the thought of riding that chairlift again, I wanted to go with him. It felt too good being around him, and after the rollercoaster of emotions and orgasms I'd ridden over the last couple days, I needed to make sure we made sense outside of the bedroom.

I felt like I was watching Derek through new eyes. He was no longer the cute, jock-y, ski bum that lived next door to Kelsey; he was *my* Derek. As long as I would have him, he was mine. I'd sear that moment forever in my mind and its memory would keep me warm for years to come, I decided.

He sauntered through the ski lodge like the

grand marshal of a parade, waving hello and palling around with almost everyone we passed. Derek was in his element. Clearly, he was adored by everyone that knew him. It was a little intimidating, especially as I started to notice more acutely just how many women clocked him as he walked by. Some knew him by name and said hello, others just watched longingly, their eyes following him.

Just as he helped me clip into my skis outside, Irina of all people sashayed over to us. "I didn't know you were working today," she said, her lips pouting. "You never called . . ." She took another step and tipped her chin towards him, closing the distance between them. It was as if I was invisible.

"I'm not working. Here to ski for fun." He gave a curt smile, trying to brush her off.

But Irina wouldn't give up that easily. "With her?" Her eyes narrowed at me, finally acknowledging my presence. "Aren't you a little *advanced* for that?"

My mouth fell open and I let out a cackling laugh, unable to stifle it. She was so brazen, so bold, and so rude that it was comical at this point. She sneered as I caught my breath. Derek stood watching me, bemused but trying to be polite. The resort was still his place of work, even if he was here today for fun.

"Oh, I wouldn't say I'm too advanced for Annie. You should *see* some of the stuff this girl can do." He smirked, his eyes dancing over me. I flashed back to the other night, my mouth on him, and blushed as warmth spread between my legs. My lips curled into a smile as I forced myself to look Irina in the face. She looked at me, then at Derek, full of disdain.

She let out a sigh of defeat and rolled her eyes. "Well, have a good day then," she grumbled as she turned on her heel.

"You too!" Derek called out after her, his voice bright and chipper. He turned to me and laughed, shaking his head in disbelief, before rubbing my shoulder reassuringly. "Ready to do this?"

I nodded and let him lead me to the chairlift. This time we went up to the Lazy Susan run, skipping the bunny hill altogether. As the chair scooped us up, my stomach churned nervously. But Derek squeezed my thigh and kept his arm across my lap firmly. I let out a slow exhale and began to feel better.

Below us, skiers and snowboarders were carving into the face of the mountain, fine mists of snow spraying as they moved. A snowboarder in a bright aqua jacket cut a sharp left and headed for a small jump. He lifted into the air, grabbing his board in hand briefly, before slamming back into the powder in a tumble. He rolled like a tire a few feet down the slope. "Oh my god," I gasped.

The snowboarder popped back up as his friend caught up to him. They both laughed and continued back down.

"It usually looks a lot worse than it actually is," Derek said.

My hand was still clapped over my mouth in shock. "Oh . . ."

"We'll go as slow as you want."

I nodded. And as the chairlift reached the top, Derek guided me off and out of the way of a cluster of eager skiers.

"Let's practice stopping with your skies parallel. I think you can do it."

"No more pizza?"

He shook his head and smiled. "Nope. I think you're ready for French fries."

"French fries?"

He chuckled. "That's what we call it when we teach kids. They love a food metaphor."

I giggled. "Okay, French fries it is . . . and how do I do that?"

Derek took me slowly down the mountain, practicing stopping and starting. It was all about balance. I had to pick up speed to keep my skis parallel while maintaining balance on my outside leg as I turned. When my skis were in line with each other, I could stop if I dug into the snow with my outer ski, while still managing to hold my balance. I fell over a couple times, but we were going so slowly, and the snow was soft, that it wasn't as terrifying as I thought it would be. With each try, I got more comfortable and confident.

"You're doing amazing, babe!" *Babe*. Derek smiled and nodded at me encouragingly.

We reached the bottom of the mountain, and my legs were already sore, but I was proud of myself. "I did it!" I couldn't help but smile as an unexpected wave of adrenaline hit me. I'd tackled something I thought I'd never do—that I'd never *wanted* to do—thanks to Derek. Despite the ache in my legs, I wanted to keep skiing.

We did another run. And then another. I was tired but exhilarated. Our fourth time up the chairlift, I leaned into Derek and sighed. "Thanks."

"For what?"

"For taking me out of my comfort zone and encouraging me so much. I really didn't think I was going to like it, but you made me feel safe enough to have fun." I tilted my chin up to him and he looked down at me, his eyes round and sweet behind his tinted goggles.

"I'm glad you feel safe with me." His lips curled into a small smile. "That makes me feel really good."

"Me too."

"And I'm really glad you're having fun. I knew you would." He grinned as he lifted the lap bar up, and we slid off the chair.

Down the slope we went. I was far more confident this time and let myself really go for it, abandoning all my doubts and fears. The wind whipped my hair as I gathered speed, my hips swishing back and forth, carving tighter and tighter zigzags into the snow. Derek cheered alongside me, grinning proudly, and calling out words of encouragement. The towering evergreens and pines whirred by, silently bearing witness to me conquering my fears. With Derek by my side, I felt braver and more fearless than ever before.

I landed at the bottom of the slope, skis parallel. "Oh my god," I murmured, catching my breath.

"That was amazing, Annie!" Derek leaned in, balanced expertly on his skis still, and planted a kiss on my lips.

I blushed and caught sight of Irina, sitting by the outdoor firepit, scowling in our direction.

"You don't normally kiss your students, right?"

Derek laughed, his head thrown back, blonde

hair shaking. "No. Never." He stole another kiss, his face spread wide into his signature boyish grin—somehow both cocky and sweet.

"Good. Let's keep it that way," I teased.

"Agreed. Plus, you aren't my student. You're my girlfriend."

"Your girlfriend?" My jaw nearly dropped open. I hadn't expected him to say that, but I liked the way it sounded coming out of his mouth. "Your girlfriend," I repeated, practically incredulous.

"Yes, my girlfriend." He smirked. "That okay with you?"

I nodded. "Mhmm." My smile was now permanently etched into my face.

"Good." He clipped out of his skis and walked over to me. Kneeling in front of me, he unclipped my boots, looking up at me with those pale blue eyes that drove me wild. He helped me out of my skis, and I never thought that could be so sensual. But with Derek's eyes on me, him kneeling before me, it left me feeling breathless. He skated his gloved hands up my snowsuit—again, who knew that could be sexy? And leaned into me, curling his arms around my waist.

He lifted his goggles, then mine, and drew my lips to his. He kissed me sweetly, deeply. If we hadn't been in the middle of a ski resort, I would have pushed him right there into the snow and had my way with him. Every touch, every kiss left me wanting more of Derek. It was intoxicating.

"How long is the gondola ride? The one that goes to the biggest peak?"

Derek's eyes lit up. "About 20 minutes." He smirked mischievously and took my gloved hand, leading me towards the line for the gondola.

"Don't we need our skis?"

"Nah, no time to deal with those." He smiled back at me as he tugged me along.

I giggled conspiratorially.

The lift operator fist bumped Derek and let us onto a gondola, not seeming to even clock that we didn't have skis. As the gondola began to ferry us up the mountain, Derek wrapped his arms around my waist and pulled me to him. I kissed him as my fingers curled around the back of his neck.

"Annie, what about the whole heights thing?" Derek asked, his voice thick and hushed.

I pushed my body into his hard. "Just fuck me so hard I forget." *Who was I?!*

He let out a low desperate growl as he yanked the strap of my ski bibs off. He lifted the layers of my clothing to expose my breasts and began to suck and nibble. I skated my hands over his front and undid his snow pants, as he sprung free.

Standing up, he grabbed my waist and spun me around, so I faced the glass—*thank god it was tinted*. He pulled my bibs to my thighs and slid inside me. I gasped as he groaned. His hands gripped my hips tightly. With each thrust, I mewed. My skin tingled as pleasure flowed into every part of my body, every toe, every finger; it pooled in my curves. "Derek," I bit out.

He plunged deeper into me and groaned. Sweat had clung to my hairline as our body heat overtook the gondola.

"Faster," I panted. "I'm gonna come."

He thrust his hips faster as I moaned, the pressure inside me mounting. I cried out as I came. Derek dug his fingertips into my hips as he groaned, coming right after me.

Our ragged breaths punctuated the silence until I began to giggle. "I can't believe we just did that."

Derek grinned and kissed me sweetly. His brow was slick with sweat. "I can . . . and I think it worked."

"What worked?"

"Fucking you so hard you forgot about the height."

My mouth flew open. "Oh my god, I totally forgot. It didn't even occur to me . . . I was so caught up in the moment." I glanced out the gondola window and over the tree line, nothing but snowy mountains as far as the eye could see. We were so high up that we were passing by the tops of other chairlifts. Eager skiers and snowboarders were gliding off them and swooping down the mountain runs.

"Good . . . let's grab a bite to eat at the top. We're almost there."

"There's a restaurant up there?!" I pulled my bibs back up and zipped my jacket up.

Derek chuckled and nodded as he bundled back up. "Yep. Let's get you some celebratory hot chocolate."

A thought suddenly occurred to me. "Wait—we don't have skis. How will we get back down?"

"We can take the gondola back," he said with a laugh. "It's not like the chairlift." He kissed my forehead sweetly as the concern was wiped from my face.

"Oh. Good." I let out a long sigh. "Hot chocolate sounds delicious."

Chapter 15

I PACED AROUND THE GUEST ROOM, LISTENING TO MY mom on the other end of the phone squeal with delight at the news that I, officially, had a boyfriend. But the more time I spent alone in this room, listening to her excitement, doubts began to bubble up.

"Mom, I don't even live here though . . ."

"So? Move! What's keeping you in New York anyway? You could raise your kids with Kelsey. Imagine that!"

"Mom, mom, mom—"

"I could move out there like Dina did and help you. Free babysitting whenever you need it—"

"Mom!"

"What?"

I laughed, shaking my head. "You are getting way too ahead of yourself."

"I can't even remember the last time you had a boyfriend! That Lee boy never even asked you to be his girlfriend." She let out a loud sigh. "I'm just excited, sweetie. That's all."

"I know, I know . . . but this is very new. And I love New York. It's been great staying in Moose Creek the past few weeks, but my life is *there*. What if this is just a holiday fling that got carried away? We haven't even talked about the logistics of being long distance yet."

"Well, you better do that soon! Time's a ticking!"

"I know. I at least have to stick around until next weekend when the festival opens. Then I'll probably head back to New York." The thought of leaving Derek punched a sinking, sickening hole in my gut. We'd been having so much fun in the moment that we hadn't addressed the elephant in the room: the distance. I thought I just had to worry about all his female admirers, but now that seemed silly when compared to the major issue of living in different states—hell, different time zones. Could long distance really work?

"Well, don't wait too long to talk to him, sweetie."

"Okay."

"I've gotta run. I'm heading to Cindy's for wine night."

"Have fun. Love you."

"Love you too, dear. Bye now," she said, hanging up.

I slumped down on the bed and rubbed my temples, feeling torn. Derek was unlike any guy I'd dated before, and I really, *really* liked him. And I liked who I was with him. But was it even sustainable? Had I let things go too far without realizing the implications and consequences? If things fell apart when I went back to New York, I'd be devastated. And what if another woman came through town and caught Derek's eye? Would I be able to trust him to be faithful? Questions and doubts swirled in my brain, causing whiplash.

My head and my heart were all over the place, and I didn't want to deal with either one. I just wanted to be in the moment and enjoy what time I did have with Derek. I didn't want to think about the what-ifs and the risk of heartbreak and betrayal, no matter how much those worries tried to creep in.

I padded downstairs and joined Kelsey on the couch, wrapping a blanket around me. Noah was already asleep upstairs in his crib, and Kelsey had propped the baby monitor up on the coffee table, facing her.

"You okay?"

"Yeah, just talked to my mom on the phone." I sighed. "She's *very* excited about Derek."

"As she should be. He's good for you." Her smile faded as she clocked my hesitant face. "What's wrong? Don't you think he's good for you? You were on cloud nine like two hours ago after skiing with him!"

"I know, I know. I have emotional whiplash."

"What happened?"

"I just don't know if this could actually work. I don't live here, and we haven't even talked about long distance. And Derek has a lot of beautiful women around him all the time, salivating over him like a prime cut of steak." I let out a soft, sad laugh. "It just feels like it's doomed."

Kelsey balked. "It's not doomed. If he's been happily single for years, with plenty of options and opportunities to date, it must mean something that he wants you to be his girlfriend. It's not like he randomly threw a dart and it landed on you and now he's stuck."

"What?" I laughed and shook my head.

"You know what I mean . . ."

I nodded and sighed. "Yeah, I know. But maybe

we just got carried away, caught up in the moment."

"Maybe." Kelsey said with a slight shrug. "But I don't think so. He's smitten."

"Yeah . . . so am I." I groaned. "This sucks! I hate having feelings!" Kelsey and I laughed as I leaned back into the couch, our bodies arranging around each other like old puzzle pieces. We each had a blanket, our socked feet tangled together familiarly, and spent the rest of the night in comfortable silence watching old episodes of *Sex and the City*, just like we did when we lived together years ago. I was grateful to turn off my brain for a while and just be with Kelsey.

Monday morning, I sat in on a meeting with the entire festival team in the lodge's largest conference room. Kelsey and her coworkers sat on one side of the table, and several people I didn't know or recognize were scattered around as Cash stood at the front. I slipped in next to Kelsey. The nicest of her coworkers, Ellie, smiled hello. The other two just glanced at me before turning their attention back to Cash, waiting for him to begin.

"All the merch came in this morning with your

design on it. It looks so good," Kelsey whispered, nodding towards Cash.

I looked up and he gave me his best Hollywood smile. He was wearing a forest green beanie with the new logo embroidered on it. I grinned. It looked so good. He pointed to his head and nodded knowingly.

"Looks great," I said, still beaming. Seeing it in the flesh, on an actual hat I could buy and wear on my own head, was so cool. I swelled with pride. I'd drawn that! And they liked it. And soon, I'd be seeing it everywhere as cinephiles descended upon Moose Creek for their first ever film festival.

"Thanks to you!" Cash winked and then cleared his throat, silencing the rest of the room that had been in a low chatter. "Hello everyone! Thank you all so much for taking the time to meet with me here today. I know we are down to the wire. The festival opens in a few short days, with the opening reception kicking off Thursday night downstairs." A collective murmur of excitement rippled through the room. "So, we just need to go over some final details and make sure everything is locked in place and ready to go. It's going to be a hectic, but exciting, week."

Turns out, the meeting had nothing to do with me, other than when they showed off the new merchandise and brand assets featuring my design. It looked great. At the end of the meeting, as people were filing out, Cash pulled Kelsey aside. She glanced at me, grinning, and I gave her an excited nod before slipping out the door.

I stood in the hallway, anxiously waiting for Kelsey to come back out when Ellie came up to me, a shy smile on her face.

"Hey," I said.

"Hey, just wanted to say I love your design."

"Thanks, Ellie. I really appreciate that." She nodded politely and then kept walking. I bet Kelsey would be a great mentor for her. She seemed like a sweet girl that could use a cheerleader like Kels.

Kelsey padded out of the conference room, beaming. She raised her eyebrows and leaned into me, her voice an excited whisper. "We're going to lunch later! I can't believe I'm going on a date with *the* Cash Taylor!"

"Oh my god, Kels!" We both resisted the urge to squeal and wave our arms in the air. This was Kelsey's place of work, after all.

"Do I look okay?"

"You look gorgeous, like always."

I knew her face would be plastered into a smile for the next hour, and that made me happy. She deserved some romance after going through hell with Rick.

"You gonna stop and say hi to Derek on the way out?" she asked as we walked towards her office.

My stomach fluttered at the mention of him, but I shook my head. "I don't wanna bother him while he's at work." Kelsey narrowed her eyes at me. I sighed. "Fine, I'm still feeling weird about everything. I'll see him tonight, and we'll talk."

"Okay, good. You'll feel better when you do." She patted my shoulder and said goodbye. I quickly made my way down the stairs and through the lodge, worried I might run into Derek, or Irina, and managed to make a clean getaway.

LATE THAT AFTERNOON, DEREK TEXTED ME AND asked if I wanted to come over and hang out. He'd just gotten off work and was going to hop in the hot tub. I threw on my red one-piece swimsuit, with the high cut legs and plunging neckline—because why not—and headed over. Coyote greeted with me with a lick on the cheek, tail wagging frantically.

"What about me?" Derek asked, pretending to pout.

I gave Coyote a good, final scratch before

winding my arms around Derek and kissing him. "Better?"

He nodded. "Much." Another kiss. "The hot tub is on and ready for us," he said, unzipping my coat. "Jesus Christ, Annie." His eyes glided up and down my body, his eyes glazing over. I'd worn just my swimsuit underneath, and he clearly hadn't been expecting that.

I giggled and took a step closer. "We should probably go ahead and get in before you get too excited," I said, glancing down at his swim trunks which were beginning to tent.

He nodded, adjusting himself, and led me out to his back deck. I ran on tiptoes and slid into the steaming water. The air was so frigid, I didn't care that the water stung at first. He slowly lowered himself down into the jacuzzi as his eyes traced the curve of my breasts. I loved the way he looked at me. I'd never felt sexier than when I was the object of his affection.

In the tub, we played footsie and talked about our days. I thought I'd be able to avoid mentioning Cash directly, but Derek wasn't going to let that happen. "Was Cash at the meeting?" he asked, studying my face for a reaction.

"Of course. It's *his* festival."

"I bet he was happy to see you. Did you all talk about your date?"

"I told you, it wasn't a date!"

He smiled, his face softening. "I know, I know. I'm just giving you a hard time."

"That's not the kind of hard time I like getting from you," I teased.

He raised his eyebrows. "Don't worry, I'll give you more of that hard time later." A tingle went down my spine as he smirked. "But did he flirt with you at all?"

"Derek . . ."

"What? I'm just curious!"

"Women flirt with you all the time."

"So, he did then."

"No, he did not . . . he actually likes *Kelsey* and asked *her* to lunch! Now, *that's* a date."

"Oh . . . good. That's great!" He looked relieved.

Derek glided his hand over the surface of the hot water, watching pensively as it rippled in his wake. "I know it's probably weird and might make you uncomfortable that I've been with so many women . . . and it might not seem it, but I get insecure too . . ."

I placed my hand on his knee under the water and leaned in, coaxing him to look at me. His pale eyes were round and searching. It was the most vulnerable I'd ever seen him look. "What do you get insecure about?" I asked softly.

"I . . . I get worried that I'm not good enough for someone like you . . . that the woman I want will realize that and bail." He chewed his lip, brow furrowed, and then sighed. "The last woman I seriously dated—Soph—she left. And I was so broken. I'd loved that woman *so* much and had given her everything I had to give, and it wasn't enough. It's cliché to say, but I didn't think . . . this would happen again."

I slid across the hot tub, next to Derek, and cupped his face in my hands. "You are enough. And any woman would leap at the chance to be with you."

"I only want one woman." He pressed his lips into mine gently. "All of those other women . . . they were just fun distractions, escapes . . . whatever you want to call it. It wasn't real; it wasn't like this."

"How do you know this is so real, Derek? How are you *so* certain about me?" I searched his face, pleading for some concrete answers that would ease my worries.

"I just . . . feel it, I don't know how else to put it. I don't know that you can quantify love like that. I just know it in my gut and in my heart. As cheesy as that sounds." He let out a low chuckle that made my heart swell.

"But we don't even live in the same state. Logistically, how could this even work?"

"Annie, are you trying to talk yourself out of this?"

"No!" I blinked back tears. "I just . . . I'm worried this might be a passing fling for you, and when I go back to New York this weekend, it will just crumble and fall apart and I'll be devastated." I swiped at my cheek as a tear started to trickle down my face. "And you're right, I feel it, too. Whatever this is, I feel it. And I don't want to lose it, but I'm afraid."

"Annie . . ." Derek whispered, leaning into me. He pulled me into his lap, wrapping his arms around me as he kissed each tearstained cheek. "We'll make it work. I'll figure it out. There's no way in hell I'm going to lose you."

I pressed myself into him and kissed him hard, like I needed to taste every inch of his lips. He slipped his tongue inside my mouth, and we kissed deeply, our arms wrapped around each other tightly like we were holding on for dear life. We kissed for what felt like hours, until our fingers and toes were prunes. When we finally came up for air, Derek grabbed a towel and draped it over me as he led me by the hand inside and up to his bedroom.

He peeled off my swimsuit as I untied his swim trunks. Our lips never left each other's skin as he pushed me onto his bed. I pulled him into me and we both gasped. Our bodies tangled together as we made love slowly and deeply. It wasn't the frantic passion of the gondola or the thrill of our first time together; this was something more. It felt like we were melting into each other, and I never wanted to not feel like this. I *wanted* Derek. I *needed* Derek . . . Oh my god, I *loved* Derek.

Chapter 16

THE NEXT MORNING, I WOKE UP IN DEREK'S BED alone—*again*. We'd made love most of the night. And yes, I know how cheesy that sounds. And yes, I might have had Spice Girl's "When 2 Become 1" playing in my head on a loop as I propped my head up and listened for signs of life downstairs.

"Derek?" I called out.

I heard a commotion and Coyote appeared in the doorway, tail wagging. He jumped into bed and began licking my face. I gave him a good scratch, and as tempted as I was to lie back down and snuggle Coyote, I needed to find Derek. I was a woman on a mission. Every cell in my body was screaming at me: *I love Derek.* I was done denying myself this chance at real love, a real relationship with a man that loved me in return. Derek made

me feel electric and alive, but also safe and cared for
. . . I didn't want to lose him just because I was
afraid of getting hurt again.

Throwing a sweater on, I padded downstairs
and found a note on the kitchen counter for me:
"Had to leave early for work and didn't want to
wake you." I briefly considered making myself
coffee but decided the matter at hand was far too
urgent. I had never been so certain of something in
my life! I *LOVED* Derek, and I needed to tell him.

I was worried that if I kept fighting it, I'd push
him away, and once I left for New York, it would all
be over for good. Rifling through Derek's clothes, I
found a pair of sweatpants and tugged them on,
tying them tight around my waist. I was swallowed
by the excess fabric but didn't care. I threw on my
coat and rushed out the door on a wave of adrenaline and oxytocin.

I practically jogged into the Moose Creek
Mountain Resort lodge, swiveling my head around,
desperately looking for Derek. People gawked at
me, but I didn't care. Sure, I looked out of place
draped in clothes five sizes too big, frantically
looking around.

"Frank!" I called out, running up to the bar
where he was restocking sugar packets for morning
coffee.

"Annie . . . are you okay?" He looked me up and down, bewildered by my appearance and demeanor.

"Yes! Do you know where Derek is?"

"No idea. Check with the ski school."

"Thanks!" I cried out behind me as I ran for the hallway. I darted around people heading for the slopes, lugging their skis and snowboards, and made my way to the ski school reception.

"Hello ma'am, how may I help you?" The receptionist said with a polite smile as she studied my outfit.

"Shelby! Hi, it's me! Annie!"

"Um, hello . . ." Clearly Shelby did not remember me.

"Hi! Where's Derek?"

"I'm sorry, but he's in the middle of a lesson."

"I need to speak with him!"

"Not again . . ." Shelby said under her breath as she shifted her weight.

"No, no, no, not like that . . . um, it's a personal issue that requires immediate attention."

Shelby stared at me blankly.

"These are his clothes? See?" She furrowed her brow. "I just mean, like, I'm not some crazy lady obsessed with taking a ski lesson with him just so I can bone him like those other women."

"Um . . ."

"I came from *his house*! He's *my boyfriend*!"

"Okay, well, either way, you'll have to wait till he's off the mountain and done with his lesson to talk to him." She gave me a forced, tight smile. I'd been dismissed, and I wasn't going to take it.

"Okay, thanks anyway, Shelby . . ." I said as I turned on my heel.

If Derek was on the mountain, then I would just have to meet him there. Heights be damned! Skiing be damned! I'd never felt so exhilarated in my life.

I grabbed some rental gear from the shop and headed outside. As I scanned the different chairlifts, it suddenly occurred to me that I didn't know which run he was even on. How on earth would I be able to find him?

I sat down on a bench by the fire pit and searched the bunny hill ahead of me, praying he was up there. It was the only run you could see in its entirety from here. Refusing to give up, I sat watch like a guard dog in the freezing cold, until my eyes fell upon a familiar lime green marshmallow. I could pick out those bibs from a mile away.

"Derek!" I called out as I stood up excitedly and waved my arms.

Of course, he couldn't hear me from there. I clipped on my skis and glided over to the chairlift.

As I waited in line behind a gaggle of children, my stomach began to churn. Without Derek steadying me, how was I going to get on and not fall off? What if I slipped out of the chair and fell to my death? I imagined sliding off and plunging to my doom and my head began to spin. *No, no, no, no, no . . . not now, Annie.* I inhaled slowly and began to take controlled, precise breaths as I shuffled towards the lift operator. He smiled and waved me forward.

The chair scooped me up and I nearly screamed. Pulling the bar down across my lap, I continued to count my breaths. *Breathe in one, two, three, four, breathe out one, two, three, four.* I glanced down and located Derek again, who was about a quarter of the way down the trail and seemed to be working with three small children on their pizza stops. *Breathe in one, two, three, four, breathe out one, two, three, four.*

The top was fast approaching, and I felt like my stomach might fall out my ass the closer it got. I lifted the lap bar up with shaky arms and held my breath as I dismounted. Gliding off, I managed to pizza my skis at the top of the hill. I was too nervous for French fries.

I looked down the wide face of the bunny hill and found Derek like a lime green beacon of hope, now halfway down the run. *Annie, it's now or never.*

With my poles in hand, I pushed off and began to ski towards him, taking care to move side to side to control my speed. *Bend your knees, eyes ahead, hold your core for balance.* I could hear Derek's voice inside my head, coaching me. *Don't lean too far forward, make sure your tips don't cross.*

My speed was increasing as I did my best to carve smaller and smaller arcs as I got closer to Derek. I kept my eyes trained on him as I swished my hips, gliding towards him. *Don't fall, don't fall, don't fall.* The cold wind stung my cheeks as I barreled towards him.

"Derek!" I called out.

He swiveled around, head cocked to the side. I'm sure I looked like a maniac, swimming in humongous sweatpants on the ski slopes. Three tiny children were all halted in front of him, their skis parked in perfect vees.

Oh god it's time to stop. I quickly nixed the idea to pizza my skis and went full French fry, shifting my weight to my inner leg and carving a hard turn. A fine mist of powder sprayed the kids as they watched me stop in front of Derek.

"Hi," I panted.

"Annie?"

"Yes."

"What are you do—"

I cut him off. "Derek, I love you. I love you more than I have ever loved any man in my life, and I don't want to lose you . . . I'm sorry I was being difficult and stubborn and scared, but I'm not afraid anymore. I just want to be with you. And if that means I have to move here or . . . ski every weekend with you . . . or whatever . . . I'll do it. *I love you.*"

Derek pushed his goggles up his forehead. His pale blue eyes were bright and sparkling in the morning sun as it danced off the white face of the mountain. I would never tire of looking into those eyes. He blinked, his mouth parted slightly, while I waited for him to say something, *anything.* I glanced down at the children, their mouths agape watching me.

"Annie, you skied! By yourself. And you did a *really* good job," Derek said, his eyes dancing over my face.

I blushed. "And I took the scary chairlift. All by myself."

Derek laughed. "I love you too. I've never felt like this before about any woman . . . I need you in my life." He punched his poles into the back of his skis and unclipped himself. "I love you so much." He stepped towards me and wrapped his arms around my waist tightly as he kissed me hard. I melted into him, letting the kiss warm me up as the cold wind blew around us.

His three small students began to laugh at us as we kissed on the bunny hill. "Why am I always getting laughed at on the bunny hill by children?" I whispered, laughing.

Derek flashed me that boyish grin and my stomach flipped. "At least this time, you're on your feet." He kissed my forehead sweetly and put his skis back on.

I heaved a sigh of relief and joy, amazed by how much I'd changed and grown in the past couple weeks. Sure, I'd be heading back to New York in a couple days, and I wasn't sure what would happen to Derek and me. But we were in love, and right now, that was enough.

THE JEEP WAS STILL IDLING AS I TOOK ONE LAST look in my little compact mirror. I dabbed on a little more of my red lipstick as Derek watched me, smiling.

"You look gorgeous," he said. His eyes were starting to glaze over.

I giggled. "Don't get worked up before we have to go in!"

"You make it hard." He smirked playfully.

I laughed harder and ran my fingers through his hair. "Can't have you going in there looking like a ragamuffin," I teased as I brushed the hair out of his face.

The opening night of the festival had finally arrived. The lodge was decked out in twinkling lights and artfully placed floral arrangements. The furniture throughout the downstairs social areas had been rearranged strategically for people to mingle easily, while leaving space for dancing later in the evening. A sea of people had flooded Moose Creek Mountain in their winter finest. I'd borrowed a fitted black dress of Kelsey's, not wanting to stand out too much. It hugged my curves and had sheer, long sleeves. Derek, in a nice wool sweater and dark wash jeans, kept his arm curled around my waist as we snaked our way through the partygoers to the bar and ordered a couple drinks. A beer, naturally, for Derek, and a dirty martini for me.

I leaned against the bar while we waited, scanning the crowd for Kelsey. My eyes found her tall blonde head bobbing excitedly as she chatted with two equally stunning women. They looked familiar; I think I'd seen them on HBO last year. When I managed to catch Kelsey's eye, I gave a small wave. She winked.

"Kelsey's killing it," I mused to Derek.

He spun around as I pointed her out. "I'm not surprised." He smiled and turned back to face me, leaning down, and letting his lips brush against me. "All I want to do is kiss you," he whispered. "But I don't want that red lipstick all over my face."

I laughed. "You'll just have to wait then," I said with a coy smile.

"It's agonizing." He smirked playfully and squeezed my waist, sending a thrill between my legs.

A hush fell over the crowd as Cash Taylor entered the room and strode towards a small makeshift stage at the front of the room. He looked sharp in a meticulously tailored suit as he grabbed the microphone, smiling.

"Hello and thank you for coming, everyone."

I glanced at Kelsey who was beaming up at him, her glossy lips spread wide as she watched him give his speech. He introduced himself and talked about the inception of the festival and how much it meant to him, and then thanked the resort and everyone who had helped him make it happen. He was charismatic and warm, effortlessly holding everyone's attention.

When he stepped offstage, he made a beeline for Kelsey and wrapped his arm around her waist, leaning into her ear. She giggled as he whispered something to her. It made me swell with happiness as I watched her like this, so excited and buoyant and dynamic. Finally, Kelsey had found exactly what she deserved.

Kelsey led Cash by the hand towards Derek and me. The crowd's eyes seemed to follow them, and I saw more than one woman cast envious looks her way . . . I wanted to laugh and shout defiantly, like *yes! That's my girl! And she's got her Hollywood dream man!*

"Annie! I'm so glad you made it in time for Cash's speech." She grinned admiringly at him, and he blushed. I don't think I'd ever seen Cash Taylor blush before. It was sweet to see this side of him with Kelsey.

"It was a great speech," I said, raising my glass.

"Thanks, Annie."

"You know, the sweatpants with your design on them have *already sold out*," said Kelsey, her eyebrows raised excitedly.

"Really?!"

"All because of your work," added Cash. "I told you the logo was going to be iconic."

"That's amazing . . . wow." I couldn't help but grin proudly. Derek smiled at me and gave my waist another affectionate squeeze.

Cash and Kelsey were pulled back into the crowd by their colleagues and peers. They seemed to be the golden couple of the evening, unsurprisingly.

Derek leaned into me, tucking a strand of my hair behind my ear. "I have something for you," he whispered. His breath tickled my ear. Taking my hand in his, he led me out of the room and outside by the firepit, which was crackling and popping into the cold night air.

We sat facing the dancing flames, as Derek turned to face me, slipping his hand into his pocket. He pulled out an envelope and handed it to me.

"What is this?" I asked.

"Open it."

I slid my finger underneath the flap and pulled out a piece of printer paper. "A receipt?" He grinned and nodded. "For plane tickets to New York?" I threw my arms around him and planted a kiss on his cheek as I blinked away tears. I could not ruin my makeup!

"I want to see your New York. I know I'm not a city boy, but for you, I want to be."

"Derek," I murmured. I ran my fingers through his hair. "You don't need to change. I love you just the way you are."

He smiled sweetly. "I know that. But I want to try New York. For us, for our future."

"Derek, I love Moose Creek. Like, *really* love it. It's wild to say, but . . . I feel at home here."

"You do?"

"Yeah . . . I could see my life here. With you."

He threaded his fingers in between mine and kissed my lips softly, then deeply. "I love you. I don't care where we end up. I just want to be with you."

"Same." With Derek's arms wrapped around me and his lips pressed against mine, snow began to fall from the sky, gently dusting our heads as we kissed. It was the kind of night that could only happen with Derek, in Moose Creek. And I knew I had many more of them ahead of me.

One Year Later

THE WIND WHIPPED THROUGH MY HAIR AS I RIPPED down *Grand Canyon*, one of Moose Creek's most advanced of the intermediate blue runs. Derek sped alongside me, grinning, and hurling playful taunts at me. We were racing to the bottom, and whoever won would have to buy dinner at Nell's tonight.

The cold air stung my cheeks, but it was exhilarating. I couldn't stop smiling as we barreled towards the bottom of the slope. We were neck and neck. I squatted down low, tucking my poles underneath my arms, and gathered as much speed as I could.

"That's not fair, you're lower to the ground than me!" Derek called out.

I laughed. "You've got gravity on your side, though, babe!"

At the last second, I pulled ahead, victorious. I'm pretty sure he let me win, but I still pumped my arms triumphantly. "Tenders on you tonight!"

He planted a kiss on me before we got out of our skis and headed inside. I pulled off my mittens and caught a glint off my ring finger. It dazzled in the late afternoon sun. Every time I caught a glimpse of the engagement ring Derek gave me, my stomach flipped excitedly. I could not wait to marry this man.

Kelsey had helped him pick out the ring, unbeknownst to me. It was a gorgeous, perfect oval solitaire—simple and elegant. Derek proposed to me in the gondola, and Kelsey and Cash were waiting at the top to celebrate with us. We popped champagne at the mountaintop restaurant with the breathtaking views as our backdrop. It might have been the best day of my life.

We walked through the lodge, hand in hand, and ran into Kelsey, who was clacking away at her laptop by the fire. "Hey you," I called out.

She waved us over. "Good run?"

"She killed me out there," Derek teased.

"What time's your flight again?" I asked her.

"8pm. Cash is on set all day, so better for me to fly in late, since he insists on picking me up at LAX every time." She smiled to herself.

Kelsey and Cash had been going strong since their first lunch date that week of the festival opening. Even though they were somewhat long distance, they managed to see each other at least every two weeks. Cash spent as much time at his house in Moose Creek as he could and when he was in LA or filming somewhere on location, he'd fly Kelsey and Noah out. He was great with Noah, and I'd never seen Kelsey happier or more in love.

"Think Noah will sleep through the flight?" I asked.

She nodded. "Hopefully. But he'll be so wound up once he sees Cash at the airport. Getting him back to sleep tonight will be the tough part." She chuckled softly.

"Let me know you get there safely." I leaned down and kissed her cheek goodbye. "And have fun in LA this week."

"Thanks, babe," she said, smiling.

"I've gotta get this guy cleaned up for our big date," I said, giving Derek a playful spank. It still felt like a dream sometimes, going home to our now shared townhouse that sat next door to my best friend's. Life was good.

"Say hi to Nell for me," Kelsey said as she waved goodbye.

"Will do," said Derek, giving my waist a familiar squeeze as he flashed me his signature boyish grin. *Damn, it still made me melt.*

Acknowledgments

A big thank you to Emily Berge for all of your help and guidance. I've learned so much from you and am so thankful!

Thank you so much to Roman Belopolsky for your incredible cover design. You are the best.

And thank you to all my friends and family that have encouraged and supported me on this author journey. I'm lucky enough to say that there's too many of you to name. I love you all so very much.

About the Author

Kit lives in Greenpoint, Brooklyn with her scruffy rescue dog. When not writing, she's dancing around her kitchen unironically to Lana Del Rey, pining for Van Leeuwen pistachio ice cream, or soaking in the bathtub until devastatingly shriveled. This is her third book.

Sign up for her mailing list at kitearnshaw.com to stay up to date with new releases.

instagram.com/kit.earnshaw

Also by Kit Earnshaw

A Violet Wind

A Crystal Dagger

Made in the USA
Middletown, DE
14 February 2022

61081195R00149